BY MONICA MURPHY

ONE WEEK GIRLFRIEND SERIES

One Week Girlfriend

ONE
WEEK
GIRLFRIEND

ONE
WEEK
GIRLFRIEND

A NOVEL

Monica Murphy

BANTAM BOOKS TRADE PAPERBACKS | NEW YORK

2013 Bantam Books Trade Paperback Edition

Published in the United States by Bantam Books, an imprint of The Random House Publishing Group, a division of Random House, LLC, a Penguin Random House Company.

BANTAM BOOKS and the HOUSE colophon are registered trademarks of Random House, LLC.

Originally self-published in the United States as an eBook by the author and subsequently released in the same format by Bantam Books, an imprint of the Random House Publishing Group, a division of Random House, LLC, in 2013.

Library of Congress Cataloging-in-Publication Data
Murphy, Monica.
One Week Girlfriend : a novel / Monica Murphy.
pages   cm
ISBN 978-0-8041-7678-1
1. Young women—Fiction.   2. College stories.   3. Love stories.
I. Title.
PS3613.U7525O54 2013
813'.6—dc23   2013019663

Printed in the United States of America on acid-free paper

www.bantamdell.com

9 8 7 6 5 4 3 2 1

"When I saw you I fell in love.
And you smiled because you knew."
—Arrigo Boito

ONE
WEEK
GIRLFRIEND

PROLOGUE

Day 6, 11:00 p.m.

Too caught up.

Those three little words ring through my head over and over. The perfect description of how I'm feeling at this very moment. Too caught up in your sweet, heartbreaking words, in your strong, capable arms, and in your warm, soft lips. I'm too caught up in this . . . pretend life I'm so completely submersed in.

And you know what? I like it. I love it. Even though I know deep down inside, it's fake. That the way you talk to me, look at me, touch me, kiss me . . . is all for show. I'm some sort of protection for you but I don't care. I want it.

I want you.

What I don't get is why we're here. Right now. I'm in your bed and we're half naked, our arms and legs tangled around each other, the sheet slipping off our bodies because our skin is so hot, it feels like we're burning alive.

You keep kissing me and whispering in my ear how much you want me and oh, my God, I want you, too, but that nagging little voice inside my head tells me we have only one more day together and then we go back to the real world.

Where you ignore me. And I ignore you. You'll get what you want—shocking the hell out of your parents and everyone else at home so they won't bug you ever again. And I'll get what I want, the money you promised me for "putting up with your shit for seven days"—direct quote—so I can take care of my little brother for at least a little while longer. We'll settle back into our usual roles.

Where you hate me and I hate you.

It'll be a lie. I might have hated you before all of this, but now . . .

I think I'm falling in love with you.

CHAPTER 1

T-minus 4 days and counting . . .

**Drew [verb]: brought toward oneself,
by inherent force or influence; attracted.**

I wait for her outside the bar, leaning against the rough brick building with my hands shoved deep inside my sweatshirt pockets, my shoulders hunched against the wind. It's cold as shit and dark from the clouds hanging low in the sky. No stars, no moon. Creepy, especially since I'm standing out here alone.

If it starts to rain and she's not done working, forget it. I'm leaving. I don't need this shit.

Panic sweeps through me and I take a deep breath. I can't leave and I know it. I need her. I don't even know her and she sure as hell doesn't know me, yet I need her to survive. I don't care if that sounds like I'm a complete pussy or what; it's true.

No way can I face next week on my own.

The music from within the tiny bar thumps loudly and I can hear everyone inside laughing and shouting. I swear I recognize more than a few voices. They're having a good time. Midterms are going down and the majority of us should be studying, right? Chilling in the library or bent over our desks, our heads in a book or hunched over our laptops, rereading notes, writing papers, whatever.

Most of my friends are in that bar drunk off their asses instead. No one seems to care it's only Tuesday and there are still three more days left of testing and turning stuff in. It's make-or-break time, but everyone's focused on the fact that we're off next week. Most of us are hightailing it out of this shit small town where we go to college.

Like me. I'm outta here by Saturday afternoon. Though I don't want to leave. I'd rather stay here.

But I can't.

She's off work at midnight. I asked one of the other waitresses who work at La Salle's when I snuck in there earlier, before anyone had really arrived. She'd been inside, working in the kitchen, so she didn't see me. Which was fine.

I didn't want her to notice me. Not yet. And my so-called friends don't need to know what I'm up to either. No one knows about my plan. I'm afraid someone would talk me out of it if they did.

Like I have anyone to tell. It may look like I'm surrounded by plenty of people I call my friends, but I'm not close to any of them. I don't want to be. Getting too close to anyone only brings trouble.

The old wooden door swings open, creaking on its hinges, the noise from within coming at me like a physical blast as it smacks against my chest. She emerges into the darkness, the door slamming behind her, the sound echoing in the otherwise quiet night air. She's got on a short puffy red coat that almost swallows her whole, making her legs covered in black tights look extra long.

Pushing away from the wall, I approach her. "Hey."

The wary glance she flicks in my direction says it all. "I'm not interested."

Huh? "But I didn't ask you anything."

"I know what you want." She starts walking and I fall in behind her. Chasing her, really. I didn't plan on this. "You're all the same. Thinking you can wait around here, hoping to catch me. Trap me. My reputation is far more outrageous than what I've actually done with any of your friends," she tosses over her shoulder as she picks up speed. For such a little thing, she sure is fast.

Wait a minute. What she said, what's it supposed to mean? "I'm not looking for an easy mark."

She laughs, but the sound is brittle. "You don't need

to lie, Drew Callahan. I know what you want from me."

At least she knows who I am. I snag her arm just as she's about to cross the street, stopping her in her tracks, and she turns to glare at me. My fingers tingle, even though all I'm grabbing at is coat fabric. "What do you think I want from you?"

"Sex." She spits the word out, her green eyes narrowed, her pale blond hair glowing from the shine of the street-light we're standing under. "Look, my feet are killing me and I'm exhausted. You chose the wrong night to think you can get with me."

I'm totally confused. She's talking like she's some sort of paid prostitute and I'm hoping to get a quickie blow job in an alley.

Drinking in her features, my gaze settles on her mouth. She has a great one. Full, sexy lips; she could probably give a most excellent blow job if I'm being honest with myself, but that's not why I'm here.

Makes me wonder exactly how many of my fellow teammates have got with her. I mean, true, the only reason I'm talking to her is because of that reputation she mentioned. But I'm not trying to buy her off for sex.

I'm trying to buy her off for protection.

**Fable [noun]: a story not founded on fact;
an untruth; falsehood.**

Campus golden boy Drew Callahan is holding onto me like he's never going to let go and he's making me nervous. He's huge, well over six feet, and with shoulders as broad as a mountain. Considering he plays football, that's no surprise, right? And I've made out with a few of the guys from his team. They're all pretty muscly and big.

But not a one of them makes my heart race just by grabbing my arm. I don't like how I react to him. I don't usually react to anyone.

With all the strength I can muster, I tug out of his grip and step away from him, gaining some much-needed distance. A sort of pleading light flickers in his eyes and I part my lips, ready to tell him to fuck off, when he beats me to the punch.

"I need your help."

Frowning, I rest my hands on my hips. Which is sort of hard, considering the stupid bulky coat I'm wearing. It's cold outside and the flimsy skirt I wear for work is allowing a major draft to coast up my legs. Thank God for wool tights, though I know my boss hates them. He says they're not very sexy.

I could give a crap about what he says when it comes to

what's sexy. My tips are still good. I have over one hundred dollars in my purse from tonight. It's already spent, though.

My money is always spent before I actually get it in my hands.

"Why do you need my help?" I ask.

He glances around, as if afraid someone might see us. No surprise. Most guys don't want to be seen with me in public.

Sometimes it really sucks, being the campus slut. Especially when I don't even go to that stupid university.

"Maybe we could go somewhere and talk," he suggests with a slight smile. I'm sure most girls would melt at first sight of that smile, the beguiling look on his face. It's a beautiful face and he knows it, with those dark eyebrows that match his brown hair and the striking blue eyes.

But I'm not most girls. I don't fall for a bunch of crap. "I'm not going anywhere with you to talk. If you have something to say, you can do it right here. Be quick with it, too, because I need to go home." I'm pretty sure my mom isn't there and my little brother is all alone.

Not good.

He blows out a harsh breath, sounding all irritated. I don't care. Whatever he has to say can't be something I'd consider. I'm too curious, though, so I need to know. Just so I can savor it later.

Drew Callahan does not talk to girls like me. I'm a local. A townie. He's the quarterback of our winning university football team. He's like a superstar, larger than life, with fans and everything. He has NFL aspirations, for the love of God.

I work a shitty job and can barely make ends meet. My mom is an alcoholic who sleeps around and my little brother is starting to get into trouble at school. Our worlds are such total opposites. I don't have a clue why he would want to talk to me.

"Thanksgiving break is next week," he starts out, and I roll my eyes.

Duh. I'm extra thankful for it, too. It means everyone will vacate this town and the bar will be virtually empty, making work a breeze. "Go on."

"I have to go back home." He pauses, his gaze cutting away from mine, and uneasiness slips down my spine. I have no idea what this has to do with me. "I want you to go with me."

Okay. *That* I didn't expect. "*What?* Why?"

His gaze meets mine once more. "I want you to pretend to be my girlfriend for a week."

I gape at him. I feel like a dying fish. Closing my lips, opening them. As if I'm gasping for my last breath, which I sorta feel like I'm doing. "You're kidding."

He slowly shakes his head. "I'm not."

"Why me?"

"I . . ." He shakes his head and clamps his lips shut, as if he doesn't want to tell me. "I'll pay you."

I cross my arms in front of my chest. They're elevated from the stupid puffy jacket. I hate it so much, but it's the warmest coat I own. I bet I look like a blimp. "I'm not for sale."

"Listen, I don't want to pay you for anything—sexual." His voice drops an octave and chills scatter all over my skin. The way he said that was sexy, though he didn't mean to be. "I just need you to pretend to be my girlfriend. We won't have to share a room or anything like that. I'm not going to try and get in your pants, but we'll have to look like we're together, you know what I mean?"

No answer. I want him to continue this so I can remember later how I had Drew freaking Callahan begging me to be his pretend girlfriend. The moment couldn't get any more surreal than it already is.

"I know you have a life and a job and whatever else that you do. It'll probably be hard for you to ditch everything and go away with me for a week, but I swear, I'll make it worth your time."

He makes me feel cheap with that last remark. Like I'm the whore every guy brags that I am. The exaggerations are out there. The stories are so outrageous, I don't bother denying them. There's no point. "How much are you talking?"

His gaze locks with mine and I'm trapped. Anticipation curls through me as I wait for his answer.

"Three thousand dollars."

CHAPTER 2

T-minus 2 days and counting . . .

> *For once, I want to know what it feels like to be someone's first choice.*
> —Fable Maguire

Fable

I still can't believe I agreed to do this. Three thousand dollars is way too much money to let pass by. And Drew knows it. He had me the moment that staggering number dropped from his perfect lips. Despite my wariness and my worry over how the heck I'm going to leave town for a week and not have my world completely fall apart while I'm gone, I said yes without any hesitation.

Guess I'm just too greedy. I can't let that sort of opportunity go, and that makes me feel like crap, despite how much I tell myself I'm doing it for my family. For my brother, Owen. He's only thirteen and I hate to see how much of a troublemaker he's turning into. He's sweet, he has a good heart, but he's fallen in with a shitty group of boys at school and he's doing bad stuff like cutting class and minor shoplifting, and I know he's smoked weed a few times. I've smelled it on his clothes.

Our mom doesn't care. I'm the only one who does. And now I'm leaving for a week. He'll be out of school for only half that time, but that's enough time for him to get into trouble.

The tug-of-war going on in my heart is near overwhelming.

"Why you gotta leave?"

I pull the old duffel bag no one's used in however long from the top shelf of the closet and toss it on my mom's bed. A cloud of dust puffs up when it lands. "I won't be gone long."

"A week, Fable. You're leaving me here with Mom for seven fucking days." Owen flops back onto her bed next to the duffel bag and starts coughing from the dust lingering in the air.

"Don't cuss." I smack his knee and he rolls over with an exaggerated yelp. "It's a special job that's going to pay me a lot of money. We'll have a good Christmas."

"I don't give a shit about Christmas."

I shoot him a harsh glare and he mumbles a halfhearted

sorry. Since when did he feel so comfortable cursing like that in front of me? What happened to the whiny little brother who followed me everywhere as if he worshipped me?

"And what sort of special job pays you so much money for such a short amount of time?" The sarcasm in his voice is clear. He's too young—no, not really, I'm just fooling myself—but I hope he doesn't think I'm off prostituting myself.

I sure feel like I am.

My brain scrambles as I try to come up with an excuse. I can't tell Owen what I'm really doing. I didn't tell him how much money I was making; he just knows it's a lot. I didn't tell my mom either, not that she cares. I haven't seen her in well over twenty-four hours, but she has a new boyfriend, so I'm sure she's with him. "I'm going to be a nanny for a family while they go on vacation for Thanksgiving break. They have three kids."

The lie falls easily from my lips, and that scares me.

Owen starts to laugh, the jerk. "You're going to be a nanny? You hate kids!"

"I do not." I so do. "The family's really nice." I have no idea if the Callahans are nice. "And I get to stay in a huge mansion."

Drew told me his family lives in Carmel. I've never been there, but I've heard of it. I did a little Google research at the library and saw photos. The place looks amazing. Expensive.

Scary.

"You won't want to leave, I bet." Owen sits up and runs his finger across the top of the duffel bag, leaving a streak in the dust. "You're going to look like a broke bitch, showing up with this shitty bag."

"Did you just call me a broke bitch?" I can't be offended, because what he says is the truth. I'm going to look ridiculous with my meager wardrobe and my torn and dusty duffel bag. His family will laugh at me. Drew will probably laugh at me. Then he'll press a fifty in the palm of my hand and drop me off at the bus station, because he'll realize quick that I make the shittiest fake girlfriend ever.

"Maybe." Owen smirks. "I hope you leaving is worth it."

Dread consumes me for the quickest moment, but I shove it away. "It will be, I promise."

"What if Mom disappears?" For a second, I get a glimpse of the old Owen. The little boy who depends on me, who treats me like his mom since ours is so unreliable.

"She won't." I already talked to her and I'll talk to her again before I leave. She needs constant hounding, as if I'm the mother and she's the kid. "I'll make her swear to come home every night."

"You better. Or I'll be calling you and begging *you* to come home." The smirk is back. "I might call you a broke bitch again and you'll get so mad, you have to come here just to kick my ass."

"That's it." Reaching for him, I start tickling his sides, my fingers digging into his ribs, the sound of his laughter filling me with happiness. "Stop!" he pants between fits of laughter. "Get off me!"

I can almost forget how crappy our life is in this one single, silly moment.

Almost.

Drew

"You're bringing someone home." My dad puts his hand over the receiver but I can still hear him. "Adele, Drew is bringing someone home for Thanksgiving."

I wince. No way did I want my dad to blab to my step-mom, especially when I'm still on the phone with him. She'd find out sooner or later, but I'd hoped for later.

"What's her name?" I hear her voice. She doesn't sound pleased. That makes everything inside me clench up.

"Fable," I tell my dad without being prompted.

My dad is quiet for so long I think he's hung up, but then I hear Adele whispering in the background. "Well, Andy? What's her name?"

She sounds like a jealous shrew. She probably is.

"Is that a nickname or what?" my dad asks me.

"It's her real name." I have no explanation for it either. Hell, I hardly know Fable Maguire. She's a townie. She's twenty years old, she has a little brother, and she works at a bar.

Fable also has pretty pale-blond hair, green eyes, and nice tits. But I'm not going to tell my dad that. I'm sure he'll figure it out on his own.

Muffled tones come across again and I know he's telling Adele Fable's name. I hear her laugh. She's such a bitch. I hate Adele. My mom died when I was like two. I don't remember her and I wish I did. My dad started dating Adele when I was eight and married her when I was eleven.

Adele is really the only mom I've ever had, and I don't want her. She knows it, too.

"Well, bring your little Fable to stay with us—she's more than welcome." Dad pauses, and I tense up, afraid of what he might ask next. "You're not one to have a steady girlfriend."

"This one's different." More like the opposite of any girl they expect me to be with. In my eyes, this makes Fable just about as perfect as can be.

"Are you in love with her?" Dad lowers his voice. "Adele wants to know."

Anger boils inside me. Like it's any of her business. "I don't know. What's love, anyway?"

"You sound like a complete cynic."

Learning from the best did that to a person. My dad's pretty standoffish. I can't remember the last time I've seen him kiss or hug Adele. He certainly doesn't kiss or hug me, not that I'd let him.

"Yeah, well, we've been dating for a while, but I don't know." I shrug, then remember he can't see me, and I feel like an idiot.

"You've never mentioned her before."

"What is this, the third degree?" I'm starting to sweat only because I'm lying. I haven't talked to Fable all day and it's Thursday night. We leave Saturday afternoon. We need to get together and get our stories straight, though I suppose we'll have plenty of time during the four-hour drive to get the details hammered out.

My throat goes dry at the idea of being with Fable in my truck alone for four hours. What will we talk about? I don't know her and I'm going to take her to my dad's house and pretend that we're together. We have to act like we're a real couple.

What the hell did I set myself up for?

"I'm just curious. We'll find out all the details when you two get here, I'm sure. Saturday night, right?"

"Yeah." I swallow hard. "Saturday night."

"We should be out at yet another country club function. You still have your key?"

"I do." Damn it, I really don't want to go back. Bad shit happened there. I've avoided that place like the plague for a while now. We've gone out of town for the holidays the last couple of years, spending Thanksgiving or Christmas in Hawaii at my dad's time-share. Or I stay at school because of football practice or whatever lie I can come up with that keeps me away from them for a little bit longer.

Tough life, I know. From the outside, my family looks perfect. Well, as perfect as a family can be with one dead mother and one dead sister, a fucked-up stepmother, and a cold-as-hell father.

Yeah. Real perfect.

That my dad insisted I come home this Thanksgiving sucks. Last time we talked, he told me he's tired of all of us avoiding the house during the holidays. We need to make new memories.

I don't want to make any memories. Not there. Not with Adele.

"We'll see you then." I can hear my dad walking, his feet echoing against the tile floor, as if he's getting out of earshot of Adele. "This Thanksgiving will be good, son. You'll see. The weather's supposed to be nice and your mother seems much healthier."

"She's not my mother," I say through clenched teeth.

"What?"

"Adele's not my mom."

"She's the only mother you've ever really had." *Great.* Now he's offended. "Why can't you just accept her? My God, she's been part of your life for so long."

The most fucked-up part of my life, not that I can reveal that to my dad. If he didn't figure everything out then, he sure as hell couldn't conceive of it now.

"I don't like how easily you forget my real mom. I don't ever want to forget her," I say vehemently.

He remains silent for a while and I stare out the window but see nothing. It's dark, raining lightly, and the wind is at it again, whipping the bare branches of the trees that dot the open courtyard of the apartment complex I live in back and forth. I can see them swaying in the darkness.

People think my life is so amazing. It's fucking not. I study hard and play harder because it helps me forget. I have friends, but not really. Most of the time, I'm alone. Like now. I'm sitting in my room in the dark. Talking to my dad and wishing like hell I could tell him the truth.

But I can't. I'm trapped. I need a buffer to get me through what could end up being one of the worst weeks of my life. Thank God for Fable. She has no clue how much she's helping me.

She can never know, either.

CHAPTER 3

Travel day (doesn't count)

> *Only a fool trips on what's behind him.*
> —Unknown

Fable

His truck is nice. Like, the newest vehicle I've ever had the privilege to ride in. He looks good in it, too, as much as I hate to admit that, even to myself. But the dark blue Toyota Tacoma fits him perfectly.

Everything about Drew is perfect. The way he dresses—his ass looks great in those jeans, and I'm not even going to mention how that black T-shirt he's wearing clings to all his chest muscles. How he behaves—always polite; he always looks me in the eye and doesn't make rude comments about my boobs or my ass. And the sound of his voice—deep and sexy, the sort of voice I wouldn't mind just sitting around listening to while he talks all day. He's got perfection down pat.

He called me yesterday before I went to work to go over a few minor things. What time he would pick me up, how we needed to draw up a plan on the drive to his parents' house.

Then I threw it out there. The money. How was I supposed to get my payment? I felt sorta whorish, asking for it point-blank like that, but I had to. I wanted that check before I left town so I could leave some money for Owen in case of an emergency.

So I met Drew downtown by my bank fifteen minutes to closing and before I headed to the bar. We chatted for a few minutes, nothing major, and then he handed over the check. He was all nonchalant and stuff, like a guy gives a girl a three-thousand-dollar check every damn day of his life.

The check was written out of his personal bank account. Signed by him and everything. He has sloppy handwriting. I couldn't really read his signature. And his name is Andrew D. Callahan.

As I walked into the bank by myself and approached the teller, I wondered what that D stood for.

Now here I sit in Andrew D. Callahan's truck, the engine purring smoothly and not chugging and choking as if it might die at any moment like my mom's crappy '91

Honda. I told my mom the same nanny story that I gave Owen. Told my boss at La Salle's the same thing, too. Considering my leaving is during a slow time for business, my boss was fine with it. He knows our financial situation is in the toilet and he was happy I found such a short-term, high-paying job.

My mom hardly acknowledged me when I said I was leaving.

I really don't know what I did to make her hate me so much. Well. Hate is a strong word. That means she actually feels something toward me. She's so indifferent, it's as if I don't matter to her. At all.

"Four hours, huh?" My voice breaks the silence and startles him. I saw it in the way he jumped in his seat. Big bad football player scared of me?

Weird.

"Yeah, four hours." He drums his fingers against the steering wheel, drawing my attention to them. They're long, and his nails are blunt with no dirt beneath them. Strong, clean hands with wide palms. They look . . . kind.

Scowling, I shake my head. I'm thinking stupidly when I need to think clearly.

"I've never been to Carmel before." I'm trying to make conversation because the thought of driving this long and not talking sort of freaks me out.

"It's pretty. Expensive." He shrugs, turning my attention to his shoulders. He's wearing a blue and dark gray flannel shirt over a black T-shirt, and it's a good look for him.

God. I turn away, keep my eyes glued on the window as the scenery passes by. I need to stop looking at him. He's distracting as hell.

"So, we probably need to come up with some sort of story, right?" I sneak a glance at him—I can't help myself. With my luck, this four-hour car ride is gonna fly by and then the next thing I know, I'm coming face-to-face with his polished parents and I won't know what to say.

In other words, I need as much time as I can get to come up with a thorough plan with Drew so we sound like a real couple.

"Yeah. A history would be good." He nods, never taking his eyes off the road.

Which is a good thing, I tell myself. He's a safe driver, aware of everything going on around him.

But really I wish he would look at me. Offer a smile of reassurance. Hell, even a fake "it's going to be all right" would make me happy right about now.

I get none of that. No thank you, either.

Bogus.

"Well." I clear my throat, because I'm plunging into the cold water despite his wanting to linger safely on the shore. "How long have we been dating?"

"Start of school sounds good, I think."

His nonchalance makes me want to choke him. "Six months, then?" I'm testing him by throwing that out there. And it works.

He slides me an incredulous look. "Three."

"Oh." I nod. "Right. Well, like I know since I don't go to school anymore." Stupidest answer ever. Everyone knows when school starts.

"Why don't you?"

I didn't expect him to ask me that. Figured he really didn't care. "I can't afford it and I wasn't smart enough to get a scholarship." As if I could waste my time with school at the moment anyway. I work as much as I can. I used to have a full-time job, but that fell through a little less than a year ago. I put in as many hours as I can get waitressing at both La Salle's and at a tiny Mexican restaurant not too far from our apartment, but that's more a temporary thing. They only call me in when they're understaffed.

The money sitting in my checking account thanks to Drew will ease some of that burden, at least for a little while. I didn't put it in the account I share with my mom because I know the second she realizes that much money's in there, she'll blow it.

I can't take that chance.

"How'd we meet, then?" Drew's deep voice breaks

27

through my thoughts. I wish he would take the initiative and come up with some of this story.

"The bar," I suggest because it sounds so trashy, and I figure the only reason he's bringing me is because he wants to look like he's slumming it to his uppity family. "You came in with a bunch of friends and it was love at first sight the moment our eyes met."

He sends me a look that calls me on my bullshit and I smile in return. If I'm in control of making up this story, I'm going to make it the sappiest, most romantic thing out there.

There is no room for romance in my life. It's so stupid, but I let guys use me because for that one fleeting moment, when the guy is focusing all of his attention on me and no one else, it feels good. It helps me forget that no one really cares.

The second it's over, it's like I snap out of my mental fog and I feel cheap. Dirty. All those clichés you read about in books and see on TV or in movies, that's me. I am a walking cliché.

I'm also the town slut who's not as slutty as everyone thinks she is—again, another cliché. And I'm definitely not the girl you want to take home to impress your mama. There is nothing special about me.

Yet here's Drew taking me home to impress his mama. Or more accurately, freak his mama out. I'm sure I'm that rich bitch's (now I sound like Owen, from "broke bitch" to "rich bitch") every nightmare come to life. The moment she lays eyes on me, she's going to flip.

"I'm assuming you're bringing me home to your mom so she'll lose her shit, right?" I need confirmation. It's one thing to think it and be okay with it. I need to face the facts head-on and deal with the repercussions later. Like how this might screw with my head despite how much I need that money.

His jaw firms and his lips thin into a straight, grim line. "My mom is dead."

Oh. "I'm sorry." I feel like a jerk.

"You didn't know. She died when I was two." He shrugs. "I know my dad will love you."

The way he says it kind of freaks me out. Like his dad is probably a creeper, and that's why he'll love me.

"It's just your dad and you, then?"

"No. There's Adele." His lips virtually disappear when he says that name. And he has really nice full lips, so I'm wondering where exactly they went. "She's my stepmom."

"So you want to freak out your stepmom."

"I could give two shits what she thinks."

The tension radiates off him in visible waves. There's something going on between him and his stepmom that's definitely not good.

Ignoring his remark about the wicked witch named Adele, I forge on. "Have any brothers or sisters?"

He shakes his head. "Nope."

"Oh." His lack of communication skills could be a real problem since I'm wholly dependent on this guy for the next freaking week. "I have a brother."

"How old?"

"Thirteen." I sigh. "Owen's in the eighth grade. He gets in trouble a lot."

"It's a tough age. Junior high sucks."

"Did you get in trouble a lot when you were thirteen?" I couldn't imagine it being so.

He laughs, reaffirming my suspicions in a heartbeat. "I wasn't allowed."

"What do you mean?" I frown. His answer makes no sense.

"My dad would kick my ass if I stepped out of line." He shrugs again. He does that a lot, but I like it because it reminds me that he has those delicious broad shoulders. If I'm lucky enough, I'll get to touch them during our fake relationship over the next seven days. I'll lean my head on his shoulder, too. Press my cheek against the soft fabric of his shirt and secretly breathe in his scent. He smells good, but I want to get up close and really inhale him.

Sappiness is ready to overtake me and for once in my cynical, no-room-for-fairy-tales life, I'm ready to let it happen. After all, I need to be the best actress on the planet, right?

"Isn't that what all dads say they're going to do when their kids step out of line?" I ask.

"Yeah, but mine meant it. Besides, it's easier to do what I'm supposed to and not get distracted. I lose myself in the mindless stuff, you know?"

"And what are you 'supposed' to do?" I add air quotes like those annoying sorority girls who come into La Salle's. I really hate those girls and how they flip their hair and laugh too loud and say the stupidest things. They literally bat their fake eyelashes at the guys and everything. It's pathetic, what attention whores they are.

Jeez, I sound bitter even in my own head.

"Go to class, study, and get good grades. Go to football practice, stay in shape, play to the best of my ability, and hope like crazy I'm impressing the scouts out there who are watching me." He rattles everything off like some sort of list, his voice a dull monotone.

"And what are the distractions you need to avoid?"

"Partying, drinking, girls." He slides me another look, his features softer, the earlier anger gone. "I don't like losing control."

"Me either," I whisper.

He smiles at me and I feel it like a dagger to my softening heart. "Sounds like we might make a good pair after all."

Drew

The second the words fall out of my mouth, I want to snatch them back. We are definitely not a good pair. She's the worst sort of girl for me and I know it. It's why I'm bringing her home. So my dad will think I've scored a hot little football groupie who gives it up to me whenever I want and Adele will finally leave me alone.

Fable really is a team groupie. She's supposedly banged half the guys this season alone, though I don't know how accurate the rumors are. This is how I first discovered her existence. A bunch of guys from the team were talking about her when we were at La Salle's one night right after the semester started. After she took our table's order, they compared notes and bragged how great in bed she is. One of them even pinched her ass when she walked by, earning a dirty look from her that made them all laugh.

Her reputation—and her feisty reaction—was my first clue that she might make the perfect fake girlfriend. I don't fool around with any of those girls who hang around the locker room after practice or after a game. I don't really fool around with *anyone*. It's easier that way. You give girls a little bit of yourself and they always want more, more, more. Things I can't give them. I shut myself off to make my life bearable. I'm like a damn machine sometimes.

Unfeeling. Uncaring. Emotionless.

My dad worries about me. I know he thinks I'm some sort of pussy who can't get laid, which blows his mind. He's confronted me about it before, once asking me point-blank if I was gay.

The question had come out of nowhere and I was so shocked, I started laughing. That pissed him off more, and though I denied the accusation, I know he didn't really believe me.

Hopefully, showing up with Fable hanging all over me will end that worry.

Damn. I know I'm a jackass for doing this, thinking like this. For using Fable in such a shitty way, but it isn't the only reason she's going with me. Not that I can tell her the whole truth, but if I did tell her some of it? She might understand. She looks like the sort of girl who would get it. Who might've gone through some of the same bullshit I have.

What we really need to do is talk about our supposed relationship more. I have to stop being so wrapped up in my worry over going home and ask her more questions. "You only have your little brother then, huh?"

"Yes, just me and Owen. And my mom." Her voice tightens. I figure she doesn't like her mom very much.

I can relate.

"You don't get along with your mom?"

"She's never around to get along with. I'm always

working and she's always screwing around with her latest boyfriend." The bitterness is obvious. No love lost between those two.

"And your dad?"

"I don't know him. He's never been a part of my life."

"But if Owen's only thirteen . . ." I'm confused.

"Different guy. That one didn't stick around either." Fable shakes her head. "My mom knows how to pick them."

I don't know what to say. I'm not comfortable with the personal stuff. I have friends, but none of them are really close. The guys I hang out with are from my team, and we talk football and sports and that sort of bullshit. Sometimes we talk about girls, though I just sit there and laugh at whatever they say. I never really join in. I don't have much to add.

Here's the deal. I could have any girl I want. I know this. Yes, I'm an arrogant ass to think like this, but it's true. I look all right, I'm smart, and I play decent football. The girls want me even more because I don't pay them any attention.

They all want something. Something I can't give. At least with Fable, I was up-front with what I needed from her from the start and I compensated her right away. She won't want anything else from me.

It's easier that way. Safer.

"Can I ask you a question?" She knocks me from my thoughts with her sweet voice. She looks all tough, with the heavy eye makeup and the dark clothes, and that platinum-blond hair. But she has the most lyrical voice I've ever heard.

"Sure." I'm opening this discussion up for potential disaster. I can sense it.

"Why me?"

"Huh?" I play dumb. I know what she means.

"Why did you choose me to be your pretend girlfriend? I know I'm not the ideal choice. Let's be real here."

She must be a mind reader. "I knew you wouldn't give me a lot of trouble."

"What do you mean?"

I'm going to fuck this up—I can feel it in my bones. "Any other girl wouldn't want to just pretend to be my girlfriend. She would really want to be in a relationship with me, you know? And I knew you wouldn't."

"How? You don't know me."

"I've seen you at La Salle's." Weak reasoning.

"Big deal. Lots of guys come into La Salle's. Lots of guys you play football and hang out with go there all the time. I've hooked up with a few of them." She crosses her arms in front of her, plumping up her boobs so I catch a glimpse of creamy skin ready to spill out over her low-cut top. I don't usually slobber over girls, but there's something about this one that makes me want to see her naked. "I'm not going to have sex with you."

She's being defiant and I kind of like it. What the hell is wrong with me? "I don't want to have sex with you. That's not why I hired you."

"Hired me." She snorts, and she doesn't seem to care what she sounds or looks like when she does it, and I can't help but admire that. "You make it sound like a proper job when really I'm your paid girlfriend-slash-whore. Where did you get that sort of money anyway?"

"It's mine, don't worry." I have money saved. My dad's in finance and has made a lot of money throughout his career. He's generous with it, especially now that I'm his only child. "And don't call yourself a whore. You're not." I don't want her to feel like one. Even though whatever she's done with other guys might qualify her as a whore, sex is the farthest thing from my mind when it comes to her.

Or at least, it was. Now, though . . . *fuck*. I don't know.

She confuses me. What I think, what I feel when she's around, confuses me. And I don't even know her. I'm totally getting ahead of myself and I don't know how to stop it.

"There's going to be no sex," she says again. Almost like she's trying to convince herself as well as me. "No blow jobs, either."

"I don't want any of that." It's the truth—at least, that's what I tell myself. She's hot, there's no denying it, but sex brings nothing but trouble. I'm not about to fool around with a girl who has an easy reputation and who's literally at my beck and call for the next week. It's pointless.

Right?

"But we're going to have to pretend we like each other," I remind her. "That we're supposed to be . . . in love." The last word was hard for me to say. I don't really use it. My dad never tells me he loves me. Adele has. But her love is tainted with shitty conditions and stuff I don't want to think about.

I fucking can't think about her, or I'll explode.

"I can do that," Fable says easily.

Realization dawns. I'm such an idiot. "I'll have to hold your hand and put my arm around you. Hug you." I didn't consider that.

"No big deal." She shrugs.

"I'll have to kiss you, too." Yeah, I didn't consider that either.

She blatantly stares at me, her gaze dropping to my mouth. Is she thinking about kissing me? "I don't think that will be a hardship. Can you handle it?"

"Hell yeah, I can." I sound way more confident than I feel.

"If you say so," she drawls as she settles deeper into her seat.

And damn it, I know she sees right through me. That should freak me out.

It freaks me out more that it doesn't seem to bother me at all.

CHAPTER 4

The night before (doesn't count)

> *I want to believe in the fairy tale.*
> —Fable Maguire

Drew

As I drive my truck down the long winding driveway, the house comes into view, every single window blazing with light. There are about a bazillion windows, the house is so damn big, and it's making a grand impression. Worry slams into me and I wonder if they're home after all.

I'd hoped to avoid them until morning.

The tension coming off Fable is obvious. Reality's hitting, I guess. It's happening to me, too. That I have to go into that house and face my demons. Totally dramatic and I sound like a chick, but shit, it's the truth.

"Your house is huge," she murmurs.

"Yeah." I hate it. Losing my sister . . . the most momentously awful thing in the whole world that ever happened in my life happened here. Even though she died almost exactly two years ago, it still feels like yesterday.

Deep in my heart, I know her death was my fault. And Adele's. This is one of the many reasons why I don't want to be here.

"And it's right by the ocean." Fable sounds wistful. "I love the ocean. I rarely get to go."

"There's stairs right off our back deck that'll take you straight to the beach," I say, trying to give her something to look forward to.

The smile she flashes me eases me somewhat, but not much.

This isn't going to be a comfortable visit. I was fooling myself, thinking Fable would make it easy. Her presence will make it a little less stressful, but there's still tension and anger and sadness, too many emotions wrapped up in this place, this time of year. By the time we leave, she's probably going to think I'm completely crazy.

Will she tell anyone about me? I didn't even think of that. Proving once again that I didn't think this plan through thoroughly enough. Everything's going to bite me in the ass in the end. I can feel it. I can't trust anyone.

No one. Definitely not this girl sitting next to me, chewing on her index finger as if she's going to gnaw it to the bone. She's nervous, but she's got nothing on me.

My palms are sweating and I feel like I'm going to throw up. It's one thing to see my parents when we go on vacation. It's another thing entirely when I'm coming home and have to face the realities of what happened inside our house. Last time I was here was almost exactly two years ago.

"Are you okay?" Fable's voice breaks the silence and it's full of concern. "You're breathing funny."

Great. "I'm fine," I say on an exhale, desperate to keep my shit together.

I pull my truck in front of the closed garage and cut the engine, letting the quiet envelop me for a second. I can hear Fable's soft, even breathing and the quiet tick of the engine, and the scent of her perfume, her shampoo, whatever it is, lingers in the air. It's light, a little sweet, like vanilla or chocolate, I can't tell, and it doesn't fit the tough-girl persona she projects.

She's a contradiction, and I want to figure her out.

"Listen. I don't know what's going on, but I have a feeling this is going to be difficult for you. Am I right?" She settles her hand over mine on the steering wheel, the tips of her tiny fingers smoothing along my knuckles. I flinch at her touch but she doesn't move. I'm shocked that she's actually reaching out and trying to reassure me.

Nodding, I swallow hard and try to muster up a few words, but nothing comes out.

"I have a fucked-up family, too." Her quiet voice reaches inside of me and instantly calms my nerves. Her easy acceptance is unexpected.

"Doesn't everyone?" I'm trying to joke, but most of the time I believe I'm alone with the madness. No one's family is as fucked-up as mine.

"I don't think so. Shit, I don't know." She smiles, and it eases over my heart as I stare at her. "Just . . . remember to breathe, okay? I know you're not going to tell me what's wrong with you, or why you hate your family so much, but I get it. I totally get it, and if you need to get away from them, even for five minutes, I'll help you. We should have a code word or something."

I frown. "A code word?"

"Yeah." She nods and her eyes light up. Like she's really getting into this. "For example, say your dad is being an asshole, asking you what you want to do with your life, and you can't take it any longer. Just say 'marshmallow' and I'll interrupt him and pull you out of there."

A reluctant smile tugs at my lips. "Marshmallow?"

"Totally random, right? It makes no sense. That's what makes it better." Her smile grows, and so does mine.

"What if you're not around?" I have a feeling I'll never let her out of my sight, but I know that's impossible.

"Text me 'marshmallow.' Wherever I'm at, I'll come running."

"You'd really do that for me?"

Her eyes meet mine, and they're glowing, they're so bright. And pretty. Fuck, she's really pretty. Why didn't I realize this before? I'm attracted to her, and I'm attracted to no one. "I'm totally willing to do the job you paid me for."

The warm fuzzies are doused with a bucket of ice-cold water at her words. A brutal reminder that what we're doing, this fake relationship we're taking part in, is nothing but a job for her. "You're right."

Stupid me. I was hoping she'd rescue me because she wanted to.

Fable

This house is as big as a museum and just as cold. It's beautiful, quiet, and immaculate, with a hushed quality to it that truthfully scares me to death. The door clicks shut behind us with a finality that sends a chill down my spine, and I follow Drew down a wide hall covered with various family photos I plan on studying later. I hear voices coming from the room at the end of the short hall and then we're there. In a giant living room with an entire wall of windows that overlooks the ocean. I can see the white-capped waves from beyond the glass, and it's the most beautiful sight I've ever seen.

Drew doesn't even notice it. He's too focused on the two people sitting on the couch, both of them drawing their long, thin bodies from the plush dark-brown velvet and approaching us with quick steps.

Nerves eat at my stomach and all of a sudden my hand is clasped in Drew's, our fingers interlocking. The show of affection startles me for a moment, but then I remember.

I'm his girlfriend. I'm playing a role and so is he, and we're doing it for these very people who are now standing in front of us with expectant looks on their faces.

"Andrew. It's so good to see you. You look positively delicious." The stepmother says this and I find the compliment odd. Who calls her stepson "delicious"?

Drew doesn't like it either, I can tell. He lets go of my hand and slips his arm around my shoulders, hauling me in close to him. I collide against a warm, solid body and tingles wash over me. He's as hard as a rock, and I have no choice but to slip my arm around his waist and cling to him for dear life. Not that I'm protesting.

This is all a diversion to avoid his stepmom's hug. She has her arms out and everything but she drops them to her side, the pouting disappointment on her beautiful face clear. And when I say beautiful, I mean stunningly gorgeous. Her near-black hair is long and straight, hanging almost to her waist. Her cheekbones are sharp, her skin a warm olive color, and her eyes are espresso dark. She towers over me, and with her slender build I can't help but wonder if she was once a model.

"Is this your little Fable?" Her condescending voice sets me on edge and I stiffen my spine. Drew spreads his hand wide across the small of my back, his fingers pressing into me, and his touch is reassuring.

"Yes, I'm Fable. It's nice to meet you." I hold my hand out and she shakes it with a disdain that's palpable, dropping my hand quickly as if it's covered in shit.

What's this bitch's problem?

"Fable, this is Adele," Drew introduces us grimly. "Adele, this is my girlfriend."

He puts extra emphasis on the word *girlfriend*, and a flicker of disgust shines in Adele's eyes. As soon as it's there, it's gone.

"Drew." The man standing at Adele's side is like an older version of my so-called boyfriend and I'm impressed. Drew is going to be killer handsome when he's in his forties or fifties if he ends up looking like his dad.

Something that's close to affection crosses Drew's face and he lets go of me to briefly hug his father. But just as quickly as he lets me go, he has me again, his strong arm wrapped around my waist and his fingers resting at my hip. It's a very possessive grip, one that I can't help but find all sorts of hot, and I need to remind myself that this is fake.

Drew doesn't want a girlfriend. He doesn't seem to like girls. Makes me wonder if he plays for the other team.

I shoot a glance in his direction, drink in all that dark hair and those intense blue eyes fringed with thick eyelashes. Such a shame if it's true. What a loss for us girls!

"Dad, this is Fable. My girlfriend," Drew says again, and this time my hand is shaken warmly, though the assessing gaze his father settles upon me makes me slightly uncomfortable. I'm being judged and I know it. I'm used to that sort of thing when I'm at work because hey, guys check me out. It comes with the barmaid job.

But this older man is contemplating me in a way that's discomforting. It makes me want to squirm and get the hell out of here.

"How was your trip?" Drew's dad asks once he finally tears his eyes away from me. I almost sag with relief.

"Easy drive." Drew pauses for a moment. "I thought you two were going to be out tonight."

"Adele decided she wasn't feeling up to another country club get-together," his dad explains.

"They have them all the time. In fact, there will be another one later this week, and we want you both to come with us." She waves an elegant hand and flashes a smile, her teeth straight and white and so disgustingly perfect I want to punch them in and watch them fall out of her mouth. For whatever reason, she brings out a violent streak in me. "I wanted to be here to greet you."

"Totally not necessary," Drew mutters, his fingers digging into my flesh.

This is just so weird. No one seems to like each other, and there's this undercurrent of electricity flowing between all four of us that's downright painful. I saw a bit of affection between Drew and his dad but other than that, everyone's wary and full of distrust. It's like they all say stuff but mean something completely different.

Creepy different.

For a fleeting moment, I'm tempted to grab Drew's hand and drag him out of here. The vibe in this place is that bad.

But I don't.

"You're staying in the guesthouse for the week. I had both bedrooms cleaned and made up for the two of you," his dad is saying, drawing my attention since Adele is trying to interrupt him.

"I don't think it's appropriate," Adele blurts, clamping her lips shut. Her disapproval is clear.

Drew's dad rolls his eyes. "He's twenty-freaking-one years old, Adele. Let's give them a little privacy."

Huh. So the stepmom doesn't want us fornicating for

fear we'll be struck dead by some all-knowing God, and the dad is encouraging us to get it on by giving us a private sanctuary to escape to.

This is all just so freaking weird.

"Thanks, Dad. The guesthouse will work out great." The relief in Drew's voice is clear, and I must confess, I'm relieved, too. I don't want to stay in this house with these people. They don't seem to like me much.

Well, one acts like he might like me *too* much, and the other hardly wants to look at me at all.

"I'm sure you both need to rest." Drew's dad winks at him. *Winks* at him and then slaps him on the back, sending him a step forward with the force of it, taking me along as well. "Meet us in the breakfast nook by eight a.m. Maria is making her famous omelets."

They have a cook. I'm totally blown away. There's too much money flowing around here, and all three of them seem so miserable or brittle or so damn fake, how can they be happy? I always believed money could buy me happiness. I'm counting on that wad of cash sitting in my checking account to make Owen and me happy for at least a solid three months, though I know that's pushing it.

I'm starting to realize money doesn't buy happiness at all. And there I go again. I'm another walking, talking cliché.

Drew

The second we walk into the guesthouse, I exhale a huge sigh of relief, thankful to be out of that stifling house where I grew up. I still can't believe how Adele acted toward me, like a jealous girlfriend ready to sink her claws into Fable. Calling her my little Fable—what the hell?

And my dad blatantly checked her out. It made my skin fucking crawl, and I'm not the one who got the once-over. This is far worse than I thought it would be and I'm embarrassed.

Maybe we should leave. Maybe I should put Fable on a bus and send her back home so I don't have to subject her to this any longer. It's awful, and I don't want to put her through it. I'll even let her keep the money.

"Your parents are freaks."

Her sweet voice insulting the people who raised me shocks me so much, I start to laugh. And once I start, I can't seem to stop. It feels good. When had I last laughed like this? I can't remember.

"Are you laughing because I'm telling the truth, or because it's better to laugh than yell at me for knocking your parents?" Fable sounds a little nervous, but I detect amusement in her tone, too.

"You're brutally honest and I appreciate it," I finally

say once I find my voice again. "And I agree. They *are* freaks."

"It was so tense in there. I don't get it." She glances around the guesthouse. With its open floor plan and a wall of windows facing the ocean that's almost identical to the one in the main house, it's still impressive, but on a less grand scale. It's a lot more comfortable in here; it doesn't give off that "look but don't touch" vibe. "Oh, you have a deck outside. I want to check it out."

I watch her slip through the living area, heading toward the door, which she unlocks and opens without hesitation. I follow her onto the deck, curious to hear more of her observations on my freaky family.

She's already leaning against the railing facing the ocean, the wind blowing through her long pale hair. She reaches into the pocket of her thin black coat and pulls out a single cigarette and a lighter, her expression full of embarrassment. "I've pretty much broken the habit, I swear, but I like to carry a few cigs with me in case of an emergency."

"And what happened in there is considered an emergency?"

Fable flashes me a quick smile before she cups her hand around the lighter and flicks it once, twice. Three times before it finally ignites. The cigarette dangles from between her lips and she brings the lighter to the tip, taking a drag and causing it to light. "Oh my God, totally." She blows out a stream of smoke over the railing and the little gray cloud hovers in the darkness before it slowly disappears. "Your dad . . . I think he was checking me out."

"He was," I agree, my voice low. "I'm sorry."

"Not your fault." She waves her hand, as if waving away what my dad did.

"I brought you here. Technically it *is* my fault."

Another wave of her hand as she dismisses my words. "I don't look at it that way. I'll just say this. Next time you bring a fake girlfriend, maybe you should prepare her a little better."

I chuckle. There's no way I'm bringing a pretend girlfriend here again. If I had my way, I'd never come back. I don't care how beautiful this place is. I hate it. This house is like a prison to me.

"Can I ask you a super-personal question?"

A ragged breath escapes me. Girls—more like Fable—and their super-personal questions are going to be the death of me. "Go for it." I have nothing to hide.

Bullshit. I have so much to hide it scares me.

"Drew . . . are you gay?"

Holy hell! Why does everyone think this?

Fable

I wait breathlessly for his answer. The air is frigid, the wind whipping around chilling me to my very bones. I'm blaming the sudden inhalation of nicotine for my way-too-brash question. I could've waited at least a day or two, right? Hung out with him a bit, gotten some personal time in with him first.

My big fat mouth and my extra-curious brain couldn't wait one second longer. I had to know. It would make spending all of this time with him for seven long days a lot easier. I wouldn't have to worry about him trying to make a move on me.

Or worse, secretly wishing he *would* make a move on me. Wondering what my problem is and why he's not attracted to me.

Holy crap, he *still* hasn't given me an answer!

"Why do you ask?" he finally says, answering a question with a question, which I hate. Owen does that sort of thing to me all the time.

Plus by doing so, Drew's going to make me rattle off a list of every gay suspicion I have about him. Not that I have many. I only came to the realization that he might be gay on the long-as-hell drive to his parents' house.

"Well, you said you've never really had a girlfriend before. Your dad is worried about you and your lack of female company. I've never seen you with a girl at the bar, let alone seen you flirt with any—not that I've paid any attention," I made sure to add. I'm being honest. I *haven't* paid too much attention to him, but if my memory serves right, he's not that much of a player.

"Maybe I haven't found the right girl yet."

My heart flares with hope, which is so incredibly stupid I wish I could punch myself in the chest. Yeah, I'm a complete idiot to think I have a chance at being the one for Drew.

The hired one. That's all I'll ever be.

"Are you, um, saving yourself?" I force my voice to sound casual, while inside everything has turned to chaos. I'm twenty. He's at least twenty-one. Is there really a possibility he's a virgin? I know they're out there, but I never figured Drew Callahan for one.

His dark chuckle tells me I'm off base, and the relief that sweeps through me is near overwhelming. "I am definitely not a virgin. But it's . . . been a while."

I take a drag off my cigarette. "Why?" Whoops, there I go again! Delving into his personal life when I have no business doing so.

He shrugs, his flannel shirt stretching across his shoulders. Drew has a really fine set of shoulders. "I don't do relationships. Sex is too—complicated."

Interesting. I find it far too easy. "Maybe you're having the wrong kind of sex."

"Maybe the wrong kind of sex is all you can get." His strong jaw goes firm and his eyes darken. He's angry. I know this is all sorts of twisted, but he looks incredibly sexy. His fierce expression alone makes my heart go pitter-patter.

His answer is way too mysterious for me. "Sounds like you're *definitely* having the wrong kind of sex." I try to laugh, flicking the ash of my cigarette over the railing, noticing his undisguised look of disgust.

Drew's not laughing either. I wonder if I offended him.

The cigarette is because I'm nervous and it sucks that he doesn't approve, but I can't help it. I smoked off and on through high school because I thought it was cool and for whatever reason, the summer after I graduated I up and quit cold turkey. For the most part.

But I keep a secret pack on me at all times, like a security blanket, only pulling one out when I'm extremely agitated and I need to calm my nerves.

Like tonight. That introduction to his parents was intense. Normally I go through a pack of smokes in six months. At the rate I'm going, I'll be smoking a pack a day by the third day of this so-called vacation.

"If my dad saw you right now, he'd flip," Drew said, drawing me from my thoughts.

I take another drag of the cigarette before stubbing it out and flicking it as far as I can. Not that it'll hit the ocean, but I like the image of it, the sizzle and hint of smoke the cig lets off upon hitting the water. In reality, I'm a common litterbug and I feel like crap, but Drew's not chastising me. "It'll be our little secret, right?"

"We're going to have a ton of secrets between us by the end of the week, huh." He's not asking a question, it's more like a statement, and he's right.

"Yeah, we are." I smile at him, but he doesn't return it. Instead, he turns on his heel and leaves the deck, slipping back into the house, the door closing behind him with a quiet click.

Leaving me all alone in the cold, dark night with my cold, dark thoughts.

CHAPTER 5

Day 2, 2:00 p.m.

Love is a smoke and is made with the fume of sighs.
—William Shakespeare

Fable

Rich people suck. They're rude, they act entitled to everything, and heaven forbid you look like a poor person. I'm wearing jeans and a sweater, nothing fancy, and they all sneer at me like I'm some sort of bum. They flash me dirty looks like I crawled out of a gutter, and then they have the nerve to look scared when I approach them. Like I'm going to pull a knife on them or something and demand all their money.

This is happening to me as I wander the cute shops that line Ocean Avenue in downtown Carmel. Drew dropped me off at the top of the hill, explaining that there's an endless number of shops and art galleries that line the main drag as well as the side streets. He said I could explore the area for hours if I wanted to, and I eagerly agreed to the arrangement since I knew his dad wanted to talk to him privately.

That's what they're doing right now. Sitting in some restaurant pretending to eat lunch while his dad drills him with the "what are you doing with your life" questions, I'm sure. Luckily enough, Adele had a standing hair appointment and she couldn't go, though she was ready to cancel. Drew's dad stopped her, saying he wanted to talk to his son alone.

Her bitter disappointment was obvious to all over that one.

A shiver went down my spine. That woman gives me the heebie-jeebies. I don't like her and she doesn't like me. At all. She tries her damnedest to spend time with Drew and he tries to avoid her at all costs. I don't get it.

Of course, who am I to judge when it comes to screwed-up families? Mine is an absolute mess.

I stop in front of a store window and peer through the glass. The shoes on display are probably so expensive, I figure I can't afford to look, let alone walk into the place. Luckily my ringing phone saves me from doing something so daring.

"Tell me everything's okay," I answer.

"Everything's okay," Owen replies. Damn, even his voice sounds like he's smirking!

"Shouldn't you be in school?" It's only two o'clock. He's not out until three.

"It's a half-day today."

He's lying. The half-day isn't until Wednesday, but there's no point in getting on him about it. I'm out of town. There's nothing I can do. "Has Mom been home?"

"Yeah, last night she was there, but it sucked." He curses under his breath. "She had her new boyfriend with her."

Yuck. Glad I wasn't there. Though if I had been, my mother wouldn't have brought him around. She would've stayed at his place instead. "Is he nice?"

"No, he's a jackass. Bossed Mom around and constantly ordered her to get him a beer. I finally told him to get his own damn beer."

I sag against the wall with a groan, earning a few strange looks from passersby. "You didn't."

"I sure did. He's rude as hell and he's a drunk. Mom deserves better."

I couldn't agree with him because I don't think our mom deserves better. She's made her choices all these years and they're always the same. I've lost count of how many rude drunken assholes my mom's hooked up with. Owen doesn't see it because I've sheltered him from the endless stream of boyfriends as much as possible.

"Did Mom get mad at you?"

"She didn't say a word, but the guy threatened to kick my ass if I back-talked him again."

"Holy crap," I murmur, briefly closing my eyes. This is why I shouldn't have left. I've been gone not even three full days and everything's already falling apart. "I hope to God he didn't lay a hand on you, or I'm calling the cops."

"Pfft." Thirteen-year-olds think they're invincible and my brother is no exception. "Like he could touch me. I'd kick his ass first."

"I should come home." Panic rises inside me. I know everything can spiral out of control real quick when I'm not around. What Owen's telling me only proves it. "I'll hop on the bus or a train or whatever and come home tonight if you need me."

"What about those bratty kids you're taking care of? You can't just ditch your job."

"I can if you're in trouble. No job is more important than family." I glance around, watching the beautiful people glide past me. It's cold, fog still lingering though it's high, more like clouds, and the sidewalk is crowded with both locals and tourists. It doesn't take a genius to tell them apart.

"Stay there and earn all that extra money I'm sure we'll be needing." He lowers his voice and I hear a shout in the distance, probably one of his punk friends. God, they were probably all hanging out at our apartment and eating all our food. "Mom lost her job."

My heart sinks to the pit of my stomach. She worked part-time in a parts store at a local dealership for minimum wage. Nothing major, but we need every last dime she makes. This money from Drew is only going to last for a little while, especially now that she's unemployed. "Great. When did this happen?"

"This morning. She texted me and let me know. Said she's going to stay the night at Larry's."

"So you'll spend the night alone." Hell, no! The last thing I want to happen.

"I'm going over to Wade's house, so don't worry. I'll spend the night there." The words come out so breezily the hairs on the back of my neck stand up.

He's lying, I can tell. I'm so damn good at reading the kid I should be his mother. "You better. I'll call Wade's house later tonight to check on you."

"Gimme a break, Fable. What, you can't trust me?" He's whining, sounding again like the little brother I remember. Another sign he's lying.

"Nope, not when I'm out of town." My cell beeps, indicating I have a text message, and I pull the phone away from my ear to check it real quick.

It's from Drew. And it's only one word.

Marshmallow.

Crap.

"Hey, I gotta go, but I'm calling you later tonight and I'm going to talk to Wade's mother. To make sure you're okay and doing your homework and whatever else you need to do."

"Fable, that is such bull—"

" 'Bye." I hang up before Owen pisses me off more and I immediately text Drew back.

I can't come rescue you if I don't know where you are.

My heart is beating way too hard after I send that text. This is the first time Drew used the "marshmallow" code word and I'm worried about him. Yesterday was all about hanging out at the house. I spent the entire afternoon at the beach when Drew and his dad went and golfed at a course not too far from the house. There are a ton of amazing golf courses there, Drew explained to me, not that I really cared. I think golf's boring, but I guess Adele went with them even though she doesn't play. She probably chased after them on the golf cart the entire time.

Sunday-night dinner had been a study in weirdness.

Adele tried to talk to Drew, constantly asking him really personal questions while virtually ignoring me. His dad, oblivious to the strange vibe, kept pace with a constant full glass of wine and was slurring his words by the end of the night.

I gladly escaped right after the meal, claiming I was tired from midterms and all those papers I had to write, which was a complete lie since I don't go to college. Drew pled the same case. We both went back to the guesthouse and to our respective rooms. I'd been so tired I thought I would instantly fall asleep, but I didn't. I lay awake for over an hour, thinking about Drew and the crazy family dynamics he has going on here.

My phone beeps and I glance at the screen.

At a restaurant at Sixth and Ocean. I need to get out of here. I'll wait outside for you.

Looks like I need to go rescue my fake boyfriend from his overbearing father.

Drew

The moment I see her, I let go of the ball of anxiety rolling around in my chest with a deep, cleansing breath. I wait outside the restaurant after telling Dad I needed to use the phone, when really I just wanted to wait for Fable.

And get away from him.

She's smiling at me as she approaches, her blond hair pulled back into a high ponytail, revealing her rounded cheeks, her pert nose, and her rosebud lips. The more I look at her, the prettier I think she is. Though not just pretty . . .

Fable's hot. Sexy as hell, with a fine body that I've seen in various stages of undress since we've been staying at the guesthouse. I caught her in a towel this morning when she snuck out of the bathroom and darted across the hall into her room. She didn't even see me.

But I saw *her*. All that creamy, dewy bared skin on display that made me want to chase after her. Haul her in close and feel her wrap around me. Tangle my fingers into her wet hair and tug, bringing her mouth to mine . . .

Holy shit. Just remembering that sets my skin on fire. I try my damnedest to keep everyone at arm's length, especially girls, but Fable's already getting under my skin and making me want.

Her.

Wearing skin-tight jeans and an oversized black sweater, she looks good enough to eat. And I never think like that. Ever. She's making me think and feel things that are somehow both uncomfortable and freeing.

In other words, Fable leaves me in a constant state of confusion.

"Here I am." She stops just in front of me, her head

coming only to my chest, she's so short. I could scoop her up, toss her over my shoulder, and carry her out of here, no problem. "Ready to rescue you."

Code word "marshmallow" hadn't been used until now, so I'm pleased at how fast she comes to me. Not that my dad was being particularly bad or yelling; he just wouldn't stop asking me questions about my future. Stuff I can't answer because I have no clue what's going to happen.

I finally couldn't take it anymore and texted "marshmallow" when I made a bathroom escape.

Now here she is. Ready to whisk me away.

"Thanks for showing up."

"Is he being hard on you?"

"No, I just . . . don't want to answer all of his questions."

"Oh." That single non-word is loaded with all sorts of questions itself. None I can answer either.

"Did you like looking at all the stores?" That's what girls do. Shop, spend money, though I don't think Fable really has much to spend. Well, she does if she wants to blow that money I gave her, but I know she's saving it to take care of her brother.

The noble barmaid named Fable. Sounds like a story out of a modern fairy tale.

"The shops here are way too expensive for my taste."

She wrinkles her nose, which is cute as hell. "I can't afford to look inside, let alone think about buying anything. I'm not really a shopper anyway."

So what does she like to do besides hang out at the beach? I know nothing about this girl. What I do know, I don't much understand. We're complete and total opposites in pretty much every way.

"What do you like to do, then? During your off time?" She stares at me strangely and I feel like an idiot. "You know, like hobbies or whatever."

She bursts out laughing. "I don't have time for hobbies. I used to like to read."

"Used to?"

"I'm too busy." She shrugs. "Working, taking care of my brother, cleaning up around our place. I always end up totally exhausted and when I fall into bed, I'm already asleep." Her gaze cuts away from mine.

"Same here." I keep myself busy on purpose. My class load is heavy, though I have no idea what I want to do with my life beyond football. Hell, I know my coach is mad that I didn't stay around campus so I can practice and that still makes me feel guilty. There's a big game coming up and I need to be at peak performance.

"Really?" She sounds shocked.

I nod. "It's easier that way, don't you think? Staying so busy nothing can bother you."

65

She studies me for a while, her gaze narrowed. Percep-
tive. As if those dark green eyes can reach directly inside
me and examine all my hidden secrets.

I don't like it.

"There you are." I turn to see my dad coming out of the
restaurant, his irritation obvious. He glances at Fable and
his jaw hardens. "I thought we weren't finished with our
conversation," he says to me pointedly.

"Oh, I am so sorry—I thought you two were done."
Fable steps right in like a good little girlfriend, slinging her
arm through mine and nestling that hot body close. Her
breasts press against my side and she gazes up at me ador-
ingly. "I need Drew's help. I can't make up my mind which
pair of shoes I want to buy."

She's good. Not two minutes ago she was complaining
about how she hates shopping, and now she's the simper-
ing girlfriend who can't make a shopping decision without
my input.

"I assume they're for tonight, then?" Dad asks.

"What's going on tonight?" *Great.* I don't want to put
on a show for anyone. Bad enough we have to fake this for
my dad and Adele. It'll feel like the grand performance if
we take this public.

"A special early Thanksgiving dinner at the country
club. I told you about it the night you arrived."

No way do I want to go. Sounds like a special sort of hell. "I don't know . . ."

"I insist," Dad interrupts, wearing that expression that says no arguments allowed.

"Sounds fun." Fable tightens her arm around mine, but I hear the tension in her voice. Tonight sounds like a special sort of hell for her, too. "What should I wear?"

"Something semiformal. Cocktail casual." Dad beams, like he knows he's making Fable uncomfortable and confused, and that's so fucked-up. "I'm sure you have a pretty dress somewhere in your bag of tricks."

"Dad." I'm pissed at the way he talks to her, but how do I stand up to him? I never really have before because shit, he's my father. He's all I have in this world.

He ignores me, no surprise. "Adele will want the two of you home by five to ensure we're all ready in plenty of time." Dad glances at his watch. "I have a meeting with a client in thirty minutes. I'll see you two later."

We watch him walk away in silence, Fable still snug at my side until he's gone. She slowly pulls away and I immediately miss her.

Stupid.

"I have nothing to wear for some fancy cocktail-party-dinner thing." She sounds stressed out. "You didn't tell me to pack anything like that."

I should have. I'm an idiot for forgetting. My plan was so last-minute, I forgot all sorts of shit. "I'll buy you something," I offer. "Let's go look around. We have time."

She shakes her head. "No way. You've spent too much money on me already. I'm not about to have you buy me some expensive cocktail dress for a one-time-only event. I'm not playing *Pretty Woman* here."

Funny thing is, we sort of are. I've seen the damn movie—who hasn't? I'm pretty sure Richard Gere's character paid Julia Roberts a.k.a. the prostitute three thousand dollars for her to pretend to be his girlfriend. Bought her a bunch of clothes, too.

The similarities are undeniably there.

"I don't mind." I grab her hand and give it a squeeze. She's watching me with a funny look on her face, like she can't believe I voluntarily touched her without anyone around to see us, but fuck it.

I need her to know that not only is she helping me, but I want to help her, too. I don't want her to be uncomfortable. I don't want my parents to put her down or make her worry she won't fit in. It's bad enough that we both know she definitely doesn't fit in.

But I don't feel like I fit in here either. On the outside I might, but on the inside? Not at all. No one knows the shit I've gone through.

And I plan on keeping it that way.

We find one of those trendy expensive chain stores at the very back of the exclusive outdoor shopping center where I originally dropped her off. Fable is semi-comfortable there; she knows the store and even though she says it's expensive, it's not as bad as most of the other shops that line Ocean Avenue, so I agree.

The place is huge, filled not only with clothes, but also home stuff like bedding, towels, knickknacks, and a bunch of other pointless bullshit. Fable makes a beeline to rack after rack of dresses and she's moving frantically, grabbing one after another and slinging them over her arm, the wooden hangers clanking against each other as she walks.

"Hey." I keep my voice low as I approach her and she pops her head up, her eyes wide. "There's no fire. We have plenty of time."

She exhales loudly and shakes her head. "I have no idea what I'm doing. I'm going to need your opinion on this."

What do I know about cocktail dresses? "I'll help you," I offer because I know I should.

"Okay. Like, you'll have to lurk around the dressing rooms and actually see me in every dress so you can tell me how I look. I can't do this alone." She looks downright frightened. "Thank God they have a bunch of stuff out for the holidays. Hopefully one of these will work."

"Hi! Can I start a dressing room for you?" The high-pitched voice comes from behind us and we both turn to see who it is. "Drew Callahan, ohmigod, is that you?"

Ah, hell. My worst nightmare has come to life. I went to high school with this chick. Kaylie, I think her name is. Yep, there's her name tag with "Kaylie" written on it. "How's it going?" I offer weakly.

Her smile is so big and bright she almost blinds me. Someone's been bleaching her teeth way too much. "It's so good to see you!" She throws herself at me and I have no choice but to embrace her back.

I can feel the curiosity and irritation radiating off Fable as she stands next to me. I offer her an apologetic glance but she rolls her eyes. For whatever reason, this reunion is pissing her off.

"It's good to see you, too," I tell Kaylie, giving her an awkward hug. She withdraws from me, the giant smile still on her face, her dark eyes sparkling.

"What have you been up to? Well, besides football. You never come around anymore." Fake pout. "Everyone misses you."

"Been busy." I shrug.

"Wow, I guess we don't rate, then. Can't even make it back to your hometown." It's as if she's forgotten all about Fable, the customer she's supposed to be helping. Instead, Kaylie is focusing all her attention on me. "Can you believe I have to work here? My daddy made me get a job so

I can learn what it's like to live in the real world. Said my ten-thousand-dollar-a-month credit card statements were getting totally out of hand." She laughs.

Fable's gaping at her. I just gave her three thousand dollars that'll support her entire family for months, and this girl's acting like spending ten thousand a month on miscellaneous bullshit is no big deal. "Um, you asked if I wanted to start a dressing room?" Fable asks out of nowhere.

Kaylie looks at her, her demeanor changing instantly. Before she was the good little worker, and now she's assessing Fable since it's obvious we're together.

I hope like hell we look like we're together.

"Here." Fable hands over the clothes when Kaylie still doesn't answer her. "I would really love it if you started me a dressing room."

The sarcasm is evident in Fable's voice and I try my best to hide the smile. Kaylie takes the clothes, her upper lip curled. "I hope these are the right size for you. They look a little small."

Catty bitch.

Fable offers her a fleeting smile. "Oh, the size is perfect. I just have humongous tits so it always looks like I need to go up a size, but I make it work. Drew likes it when they hang out and he can see them. Easier access and all that. Right, honey?" She bats her eyelashes at me, and this time I can't hold back the chuckle that escapes.

This girl—my fake girl—is just too much.

"Right," I murmur, enjoying the humor dancing in Fable's eyes.

Kaylie mutters something under her breath and heads for the dressing room.

"Well. *She* was rude," Fable says the moment Kaylie's out of earshot.

"Sorry about that." I feel like I'm constantly apologizing for this world I'm from that treats Fable so terribly. It sucks.

She shrugs. "Those types of girls always work at these type of stores. They don't like me because they know I can't afford anything in here."

"Whatever you want, I'm buying." I want Fable to walk out of this stupid store with so many bags she can't carry them all. Seriously. I see the way she eyes everything in here. She likes it. She's trying to play nonchalant, but this would be her type of store if she could afford it; I can sense it.

"I only want a dress," she says, her voice small.

"And shoes," I remind her.

"Right. Shoes."

"Jewelry if you need it. Maybe a hair thing or something?" Fuck, I don't know. I don't pay attention to what girls need to get all dolled up.

"I'll figure something out. Meet me at the dressing

rooms in fifteen minutes." She offers me a sweet smile and it hits me like a blow to the chest, stealing the air from my lungs.

I want to make her smile like that at me again. It was a real one. No put-on cheesy grin for people watching or the fake you're-my-hot-boyfriend smile she gave me earlier with my dad. This smile was genuine.

Genuinely beautiful.

Fable wanders off in hot pursuit of the perfect dress. I wander the store, looking around. Starting to feel generally uncomfortable. I've never played this role before, attentive boyfriend ready to help his girlfriend pick out her new outfit.

I'm looking forward to seeing her in something beyond the casual stuff she usually wears.

"So Drew. Your girlfriend is a bit . . . different." Kaylie's back.

Great.

"How so?" I turn to look at her, seriously interested in her opinion. Why the hell is Fable so different? Hell, even I think so, but I can't put my finger on why.

Kaylie shrugs. "She doesn't look like your usual type."

I never had a type. I never had a steady girlfriend in high school. I was too busy playing football *and* baseball. I had to choose one after I played both my freshman year in college as well. Talk about having no time to date.

"How long have you two been going out?" Kaylie asks when I don't say anything.

"Since August, when school started."

"Oh." Kaylie nods, nibbling on her lower lip. It's a flirtatious gesture that does absolutely nothing for me. "You know, Drew, I always had a crush on you in high school."

Hell, I want to groan out loud, but I hold it in. This is not going how I planned. I don't want to deal with this shit. "Uh . . ."

"You never noticed me, no matter how I tried. And lord knows, I tried." Kaylie takes a step closer and runs her index finger down the center of my chest, lingering on the buttons of my henley shirt. "Wow, you're muscular."

"Kaylie." I take a step back. "I have a girlfriend."

"Such a shame, too." She's pouting again and it sucks. If she thinks that's cute, she's totally wrong. "I've always been the type to want what I can't have."

That she just admitted it shows how crazy she is. "I need to go help my girlfriend. Talk to you later."

"Let me know if she needs anything!" Kaylie screeches at me as I walk away.

Yeah, right. I'm going to keep this girl as far away from me as possible. I'm afraid Fable would've kicked her ass if she saw what Kaylie just did to me. How she touched me.

Having a fake girlfriend brings me a hell of a lot of unwanted attention.

Fable

After trying on a bunch of dresses for almost thirty minutes, I finally find the perfect one. It's like I knew it would be perfect since I saved it for the very last. Drew is patiently waiting for me outside, the dressing-room attendant having provided him with a chair and everything.

I love coming out of the dressing room and showing him what I have on next. He sits there slouching in his chair, his big body sprawled all over the place, legs spread wide and a bored look on his too-handsome face. I'm torturing him, I know it, but his gaze lights up every time he sees me, even if the dress is awful.

And he's honest, too. I can appreciate that. The few that really were awful, he point-blank said they were bad. So far he likes the first one I tried on best, and I know it's a good choice, but this one . . . the one I have on right now, is so beautiful it almost makes me want to cry.

It's also, at almost four hundred bucks, the most expensive one of them all. Guilt eats at me. I shouldn't want it. It's too much money. But oh my God, it looks *soo* good on me and I don't like to brag, but . . . yeah. As I told that stupid girl who knows Drew, my tits look great in it, and they're not all hanging out and too obvious, either. Everything about this dress is understated, classy . . .

Yet sexy.

Taking a deep breath, I open the door and step out into the waiting area of the dressing room. There sits Drew in slouch mode, his gaze locked unseeingly on me. He blinks slowly and sits up straight, his eyes going wide as he drinks me in.

"Damn," he breathes and clears his throat.

The smile that teases the corners of my mouth can't be contained. I do a little twirl, imagining the super-high heels I'd like to buy to go with this dress. I really don't want to spend too much money on shoes, though. Maybe there's a Payless ShoeSource close by or something.

Yeah, right.

"Do you like it?" I ask when I face him once more. The dress is black and silky, sleeveless, with a lacy bodice that covers me to my collarbone. It fits close, nipping in at the waist, stopping about mid-thigh, revealing lots of leg. The best part is the back. It does a deep vee, trimmed in black velvety lace, and exposes a lot of skin. No way can I wear a bra with it.

"Get it," he says without hesitation. "You look . . ."

"Okay? Really? It's kind of short." I glance down at myself. "And I'll need shoes."

"Whatever you need, cool. That dress is it." His gaze drops to my legs, lingering appreciatively. "And it's definitely not too short."

Excitement courses through me. He likes it. He's looking at me like he wants me and I know it's crazy, but I love it. I want to see him look at me like that again. All night.

"There's a problem, though." I shift on my feet, trying to ignore the worry coursing through me. I don't want to hear him say no.

"What could be the problem?" He stands and approaches me. My knees threaten to buckle and I lock them, hoping like crazy I don't fall over like an idiot all because he's coming closer with that dark, intriguing look in his eyes.

Like he wants to gobble me up.

"The dress costs almost four hundred dollars," I whisper. I could buy a ton of groceries with money like that. Pay most of our rent. Buying a dress I'm going to wear one time for that much money is insane.

Drew doesn't even flinch. "I'm still getting it for you." He stops directly in front of me and rests his big hands on my waist. His touch burns through the fabric of the dress; I can feel his every finger press into my flesh, and my heart starts to race. "You look beautiful, Fable."

"I—I like it, too." I sound breathless and I want to kick myself. Guys don't make me breathless. They don't make my heart race, either.

But somehow this one does.

"Find something that works?" Kaylie is standing just behind Drew, her withering stare directed at me, and I wonder if Drew is putting on this show of touching me for her benefit.

My entire body deflates at the realization and I withdraw from his hands. "I'm going to change. We should probably get going. And I still need to find shoes."

"What's the occasion?" Kaylie sounds all perky and sweet but there's a hint of venom just beneath the surface. This girl looks like she'd love to sink her claws into Drew.

And then scratch my eyes out with them.

"My dad's dragging us to the dinner tonight at Pebble Beach," Drew tells her.

"Oh, I'll be there, too. We'll have to hook up." She giggles and I sneak back into the dressing room, slamming the door with enough force to rattle the walls.

Hook up. Nice choice of words. If she doesn't watch it, I'm going to send a right hook straight into her too-perfect nose.

CHAPTER 6

Day 2, 6:17 p.m.

> *Remember that great love and great achievements*
> *involve great risk.*
> —The Dalai Lama

Fable

"My dad is blowing up my phone," Drew calls from the living room. "Are you ready yet? They're threatening to leave without us if we're not ready to go by six thirty."

Holy crap! My hands are shaking as I finish putting on mascara and I'm afraid I'll stab my eye out. Drew's constant reminders that his parents are waiting don't help. I have never been so nervous about how I look in all my life. Not even when I attended my junior and senior proms and spent hours getting ready. Saving all my money to buy the cheap dress from JC Penney, thinking I looked all hot when I probably looked like a little girl playing dress-up.

Now here I stand in a dress, shoes, and miscellaneous accessories that cost almost one thousand dollars. Drew didn't protest when Kaylie rattled off the total after she rang us up. He merely handed over his credit card without a word, though she was quick to give me a shitty little look at the end of the transaction.

I really hope that witch isn't there at this country club thing tonight. It's going to be miserable enough without her adding to it.

"Fable." Drew raps on the bathroom door so hard it swings open and thank God I'm not standing there naked, though he knows I'm not, so I'm freaking out over nothing. He's standing in the doorway, looking outrageously gorgeous in black pants and a silvery-gray button-down shirt and black tie. My mouth dries up as I stare at him in the reflection of the mirror and he returns the same stare. His eyes are wide, drinking me in, sliding down the length of my body, and I feel his gaze as if he's actually touching me. "Uh, are you ready?" he asks, his voice husky.

"Give me two more minutes." I yank my gaze away from his and dig through my makeup bag, pulling out a pale pink lip gloss. I open it and slick it on, rubbing my lips together as I assess myself in the mirror.

I wore my hair up to show off the back of the dress, a few little wisps hanging around my face. I gave myself dark smoky eyes, rosy cheeks, and pale lips, going for an understated look. The dress is perfection—I can't believe how I look in it—and the shoes I'm wearing are daringly high. So high, I probably hit at about Drew's shoulder. Hopefully I won't fall on my butt when I walk.

The sparkly earrings and matching chunky rhinestone bracelet complete the outfit. I almost feel overdressed, but Drew's not complaining so neither am I. I'm still worried about his opinion, though, and I focus on zipping my makeup bag closed. Hopefully he thinks I look good. I think he looks gorgeous, but when does he not? The guy could wear a paper bag around his privates and make it look designer.

I called Owen's friend's mom earlier and she reassured me Owen was there with them staying the night, so I feel good about that. I tried to call my mom, but no answer. I sent her a quick text letting her know I was all right.

Still no reply. She's probably hanging out with her flavor of the month and doesn't have time for me.

Squaring my shoulders, I turn to face Drew. He's got his hands propped against the top of the doorway and he's sort of leaning into the bathroom, his shirt stretching across his chest, emphasizing his sheer size. I can smell his cologne, a clean, citrusy scent that smells so good, I want to push my face into his neck and sniff him there. Maybe even lick his skin and see what he tastes like . . .

My thoughts are getting so out of hand and we still have way too many days left. I'm going to be a complete mess by the time Thanksgiving rolls around.

You can handle this. He's just a guy. And they don't mean anything to you.

"Ready?" he asks me after I stand there silently for probably too long.

Nodding, I hold out my cell phone. "I have nowhere to put this. The purse I brought is huge, and no way would it look good with my outfit."

His full lips curl in the faintest smile. "Do you have to take it with you? You can leave it here. We'll only be gone for a few hours, tops."

"Well . . ." My voice trails off. A few hours is too long for me to be without my cell. "I do. What if my brother calls and needs help? Or my mom?"

His gaze softens, fills with understanding. "Can you put it in your—bra?"

I actually giggle. And I never giggle. "I'm surprised you know that old bar trick." I sober up. "I can't. I'm not wearing one."

He looks like he just swallowed his tongue. Just saying

that was worth his reaction alone. "I can keep it in my pocket if you want."

"Really? Thanks. I appreciate it." I set the phone on vibrate and hand it over, our fingers brushing. Electricity shoots up my arm, and I rub at it absently while I watch Drew slip my phone into his pocket.

"Let's go. We'll meet them outside by the car."

I follow him out of the guesthouse toward the giant four-car garage. These people live in such excess, it's staggering. "We're going to ride with them?"

"My dad insists." He doesn't look too pleased, which reassures me. I don't want to ride with them either. "I guess we could take advantage and get shit-faced drunk if we want."

I've seen him at La Salle's plenty of times. "I've never seen you drunk. From what you've told me, I figure you don't like to get out of control. To me, getting drunk equals out of control."

He glances over at me. "You're right. Guess you've got me all figured out."

"Not quite," I murmur as we reach the garage. I wish I did, but he's holding his secrets extra close.

"Aren't you bringing a coat?"

I shake my head, hold back the gasp that wants to escape when he scoops up my hand with his. My reaction to him is so ridiculous, and I really need to learn how to control it. Everything between us isn't real and I have to remember that. No matter how good it feels.

And my fingers entwined with his feels really, really good.

"You're going to get cold," he says as we stop in front of the garage and wait for his parents. A hint of satisfaction rolls through me because after they nagged at us from the moment we arrived home, now we're the ones waiting for *them*.

"Maybe you'll keep me warm?" With a smile aimed directly at him, I nudge his upper arm with my shoulder, marveling at his rock-hard biceps. I've been hoping to catch a glimpse of him with his shirt off, but it hasn't happened yet. I know beneath the clothes he's built like a god, and I want to see all that muscly goodness.

He lifts a brow. I really love it when he does that. "Are you flirting with me?"

I'm about to flirt some more when his parents appear, the two of them walking hurriedly toward us as one of the garage doors opens, revealing a gorgeous black Range Rover parked within. I try to act all nonchalant as we approach the car, Drew opening the door for me so I can slip into the backseat first. I don't expect him to slide in after me, and I swear I feel his fingers tickle the back of my thigh for the briefest second.

But when we settle in our seats, his expression is completely neutral, so I figure I imagined it.

His parents aren't really talking and that makes me uneasy. I wonder if they had a fight. Or if they're still pissed because I took too long. Drew reassured me earlier that the dinner didn't start until seven, so even now we still have a half hour. But maybe they like to be early and snag a good table. Crap, I don't know!

I'm going into this blind and I'm nervous.

Drew reaches out and grabs hold of my hand again and when I look up at him, he smiles at me in the darkness. I have this sudden sense that it's the two of us against the world. We're in this together and we have to depend on each other to get through it. I know that sounds completely dramatic and silly, but I can't help the way I feel.

I also can't help but stare at him for a little too long, marveling at the masculine beauty of his face. It's so unfair when people are so sickeningly good-looking, and that's Drew. He should disgust me he's so gorgeous.

Instead he makes me feel all swoony and stupid. Like my head is getting lighter from all the brain cells evaporating the longer I look at him, and I wonder if he can feel me staring.

When he turns to meet my gaze, I know he feels me staring. He smiles, the sight of it reassuring my nervous, racing heart, and I blurt out the first question I can think of. "What does the D stand for?"

He frowns and shakes his head. "What D?"

"Your middle name. You're Andrew D. Callahan." I pause, hoping his parents aren't listening to us. His dad is backing the car out of the garage and Adele is murmuring something to him, but I can't make out what.

"Ah." He nods, as if he knows an age-old mystery. "What do you think it stands for?"

Hmm, he's acting kind of flirtatious, too. I like it. Makes the moment lighter, especially with the tension-filled drama going on in the front seat. "Dumbledore?"

Chuckling, he shakes his head. "No."

I tap my index finger against my chin. "Daniel."

"Nope."

"Dylan."

"Huh. That goes with the whole Callahan Irish theme, but wrong guess."

I go through a few other D choices, all of them ridiculous, when I finally hit on the right one.

"David," I whisper.

His smile grows. "You finally got it."

"Do I win a prize?" I return his smile.

"Sure," he says easily. "What do you want?"

"You're asking me? Shouldn't you determine the prize?"

"You can have whatever you want." He skitters his

thumb across the palm of my hand, sending a flurry of shivers across my skin. "Name it and it's yours."

We haven't kissed yet. Well, I gave him a quick kiss on the cheek last night, but other than that, nothing. And that's what I want. A kiss from Drew. I'm not talking a long, drawn-out, tongue-twisting make-out session, though that sounds promising.

I just want to feel his lips press against mine once. I want to know how soft they are, what he tastes like, how warm his breath is. I want to enjoy that first, tentative, thrilling moment of kissing someone.

But am I gutsy enough to ask for it?

Drew

She's hesitant and I don't know why. Anticipation pours through my veins as I wait for her reply. I'm not sure what's gotten into me, but it seems to have gotten into her, too, and we're flirting with each other. For real and not because we have to, but because we want to.

It helps to ease the tension that's emanating from the front seat. I have no idea what those two are fighting about, but I'm not going to let them get me down. I have a gorgeous girl sitting next to me in the dark, in the backseat of a car, wearing the sexiest dress I've ever seen. It covers practically her entire front but molds to her curves, and the skirt is so damn short, it wouldn't take much for me to sneak my hand under there and touch her.

But it's the back of the dress that gets me, makes me want to peel her out of it and see Fable in all her naked glory. That low-cut vee and how it dips to the middle of her back, the way it exposes all of that smooth, silky skin, the delicate lace laying against her flesh. Shit, I'm a goner every time I look at her. My fingers literally itch to touch her there.

Touch her everywhere.

"I want you to kiss me," she finally says, her voice so soft, I almost can't hear her. In fact, I'm wondering for the craziest moment if I'm hallucinating, because no way in hell did she just ask me to kiss her.

Shooting a glance toward the front seat, I notice they're not paying us any mind. The satellite radio is going, playing some smooth jazz shit, and they're talking to each other in low, dark murmurs. They both sound pissed with each other and I wonder if any of this involves me.

Right now, I don't care. I should never care. What they fight about isn't my problem.

"Drew." Her soft voice draws me back and I look at Fable, find myself lost in her green eyes. "Did you hear me?"

"Yeah," I whisper, swallowing hard. Fuck, my parents are right there! Adele only has to turn her head about two inches and she's looking right at us. She won't like it if I kiss Fable in front of her. She might even flip out. I don't know if I want to take that risk.

Don't be a pussy, man. Kiss her, asshole. KISS HER!

Leaning over the center console, I reach out and drift my fingers across Fable's cheek. Her skin is so soft and she closes her eyes, her lips parting. Her tongue sneaks out and she licks her upper lip. Just like that, I'm sporting a hard-on, and without thought I settle my mouth on hers. Once. Softly, as light as a butterfly's wings, my lips lingering for a few, stolen seconds before I break the connection.

Her lids flutter open and she's watching me with that attentive gaze. The one that makes me feel like she can see everything I hide inside me. The good and the bad. The beautiful and the ugly. "That's all you got?"

She's teasing me. I can see it in the light of her eyes, the slight quirk of her lips. Damn, I want to kiss her again, so I do.

This time, she slips her hand around the back of my head and keeps me there so I can't escape. And I don't want to. Her fingers thread through my hair, stroking me as our lips connect again and again. Her touch feels so good. A little moan escapes me and I swipe at her upper lip with my tongue, savoring her sticky-sweet taste. She parts her lips, opening herself to me, and I take full advantage.

I search her mouth with my tongue slowly. Thoroughly.

She tastes fucking amazing and my skin is suddenly too tight; I'm burning up inside. I'm so hard, I ache with it, and I can't remember ever becoming as turned on as this and so fast, too. Our fun little make-out session is getting out of control quick, and I'm worried my parents are going to lose it when they see us all over each other in the backseat like a couple of teenagers.

Within two seconds I don't care if my parents see us or not. I'm lost in her touch, lost in the way her body molds to mine, how she tastes, the sound of her breathing.

My hand is resting on her waist, my fingers massaging the silky fabric of her dress. The road that takes us to Pebble Beach is curvy and my dad is driving kind of fast, so we're swaying against each other in the backseat. I take advantage again, pulling her closer, loving how easily she comes to me. She wraps her arms around my neck and devours my mouth, her little tongue twisting and tangling with mine.

Our kissing isn't for show. This isn't to make an impression on others. We're kissing each other because we want to. And we're not stopping ourselves, either.

We're only two days into this fake relationship crap and this is where we're at, wrapped around each other like pretzels and hoping like hell we don't have to let go of each other anytime soon.

At least, that's what I'm feeling.

The car swerves hard to the left, sending me toppling over Fable.

"Andy!" Adele chastises, and my dad grumbles a half-hearted sorry as he slows down.

I end the kiss first, opening my eyes to find Fable staring up at me. She looks dazed; her lips are damp and her cheeks are flushed. She's even prettier than when I first saw her in the bathroom and was completely blown away by the way she looked in that sexy dress.

She's prettier because *I'm* the one who put that glow in her eyes and the color in her cheeks.

"We—" She swallows hard, her breathing accelerated, and she licks her lips again. I lean into her real quick, pressing my forehead against hers. I close my eyes and count to five before opening them again, trying to gather my thoughts so I won't end up sounding like a dumbass when I finally find my voice.

"We what?" I ask, pulling away from her the slightest bit. I don't want to let her go. It feels too good, holding on to her, her curves filling my palms, her mouth fused with mine.

Holy shit, I never think like this! I usually run like crazy. Kissing and sex and all the other crap that comes with it leads to . . . I can't explain it. Sex leads you to a bad place.

Where you're doing things you don't want to be doing. Or doing things that feel so damn good but you know are wrong. Sex for me has always been . . . shameful.

I hate that. I hate feeling guilty for doing something that feels absolutely amazing. I hate being involved with people I shouldn't have been; they ruin everything for you.

That's what I despise the most. And resent. I'm full of such resentment, I'm tempted to tell Fable she doesn't want to hang around with a guy like me, even if it's fake.

Especially if it's fake.

"We should do that again. Don't you think?" She runs her fingers through my hair once more and I close my eyes, savoring her touch. I suddenly crave it. Human touch. Fable's touch.

"You mean kiss?" I ask, because I'm confused. I don't know what she's talking about, too distracted by how she's touching me, the sound of her voice.

"Yeah. We need to put on a good show tonight, right?"

Wait a minute, put on a good show? Was this some sort of practice session or something? "Uh, sure."

"Give the neighbors and your parents' friends and probably some of your friends, too, an extra-good show so they believe we're really, truly involved?" She's pulling out of my embrace and my arms feel empty. She settles into her seat, her breath still coming fast. At least I know I affected her somewhat.

"I guess." I shrug. I feel like I've been used. And that's completely ridiculous.

"Perfect." The smile on her face blows my mind. I didn't think she was this beautiful a week ago. But I didn't know her, either. She's growing on me. A lot. I want to get to know more about her. She's still a mystery, but so am I. I can't tell her my secrets, though.

They'll send her running.

Fable

The man can kiss.

Drew has no idea how his kiss shatters me so completely, I feel all raw and exposed. Vulnerable. I totally tried to play it off just now, like we're only messing around back here for the sake of our phony boyfriend-and-girlfriend status, but that's not true. That kiss had nothing to do with us pretending we're together.

And everything to do with me wanting more from him than he's probably willing to give.

My entire body is shaking and I take a deep breath. The car slows and turns onto a driveway, and I know we're at our destination. The country club awaits, most likely filled to the brim with a bunch of snooty snobs and holy crap, I'm still incredibly nervous. Oh, and amped up by that kiss. Adrenaline runs through me, making me tremble, and

I glance out the window, staring at the scenery spread out before us. I need it to distract me so I'll stop thinking about Drew's magical lips and tongue.

So I focus on something mindless. Like how we really need to take a ride along 17 Mile Drive before we leave, so I can ogle all the houses and the ocean and soak up all that beauty and wealth. No way am I going to miss seeing it, especially since we're so close. Gorgeous houses and serene yards, everything so beautiful it's almost painful to look at for too long. Yes, I should definitely focus on scenic drives and ocean views.

Not beautiful men who kiss every thought out of my head and leave me a trembling, aroused mess.

"Do I look all right?" I smooth my hand over my hair, hoping I'm not all mussed up.

"You look amazing." The sincerity in his voice touches me deeply. I am a sucker for this man and he doesn't even know it.

I glance over at him. His mouth is swollen, his eyes are glittering, and his hair is sticking up all over the place from me tugging on it. Other than that, he looks perfectly fine.

Really fine. But what else is new?

Reaching out, I smooth his hair down, combing it back into place with my fingers. I do it a few times more than necessary, but his hair so silky soft and I love how it clings to my fingers. He doesn't say a word, he hardly moves, though those intense blue eyes are locked on me the entire time. When I finish, I pull away from him, settling in my seat with a breath of relief.

"There," I say, clearing my throat when I realize my voice is still shaking. *Damn it!* "Now you look presentable."

The car pulls to a stop in front of a giant, beautiful old building and my door swings open, a man in a dark-green and white uniform with a kind smile peering inside. "Need help out, miss?"

"Yes, thank you." I settle my hand in his white-gloved one and he pulls me out of the backseat. Drew opens his own car door, as does his dad while another attendant takes care of Adele.

I hardly noticed what she was wearing back at the house, so I take my time to check her out now. Her dress is a dark navy blue, a long, slender column that skims her every willowy curve, covering her from her neck to her feet. It doesn't reveal much skin, but it showcases the length of her body, the fact that there isn't an ounce of fat on her anywhere.

Her hair is pulled back into a low ponytail, black as a midnight sky, with the ends swinging across her perfect butt as she turns to greet someone. The place is bustling with excitement, lots of people are pouring inside, and I know it's going to be packed. I really hope we have a table already reserved or something, though it might be kind of exciting if Drew and I were together but separated from his parents.

In fact, I would prefer it.

"Like what you see?"

Adele's contemptuous voice startles me and I lift my gaze to hers, to discover she's watching me with an undisguised sneer curving her lips.

"Your dress is beautiful," I say, and she smiles icily in response but otherwise doesn't say a word.

God! I want to stomp my foot and tell her to screw off. But I hold it all in, offering her a faint smile when she looks back my way. Though she's not really looking at me, she's looking at Drew, who's come up behind me. I know this because I can sense him, smell his delicious scent, feel the alluring warmth that radiates off his big body.

I have it so incredibly bad for this guy. I'm in deep trouble. What if he doesn't feel the same way? What then? There's nothing I can do about it. I signed up for this and now I have to deal with the consequences, no matter what happens.

"Ready to go in?" He settles his hand on my bare shoulder and his touch is such a shock to my system, I feel like I can't breathe, that my lungs are frozen solid.

Turning my head to the side, I realize he's standing close. *Really* close. His mouth is at my temple, as if he's kissing me there, and I can feel his warm breath stir the little tendrils of hair that rest at my forehead. We make an intimate picture to everyone, I'm sure. I wonder if it's all for Adele's benefit.

I don't understand the control she has over him. He puts up a front for her with me, yet doesn't want to be around her. None of it makes any sense.

For the majority of my life, I've allowed myself to be used. Repeatedly and by everyone who surrounds me. I should be numb to this. But I'm not, not with Drew. I don't want him to use me to make his parents freak out. I don't want him to use me as some sort of weird protection so the people in his life quit asking probing questions and leave him alone.

I want him to actually like me. I want to spend more time with him. Real time. Not phony "oh, let's hang all over each other" time either.

"Yes," I finally say in answer to his question because I don't know what else to do. We need to face reality and that crowd waiting for us inside.

He squeezes my shoulder and we walk in together, trailing behind his parents, earning a hard glare from Adele as we pass through the open double doors.

This night is going to feel like an eternity. It already does.

CHAPTER 7

Day 2, 9:38 p.m.

I've never dropped anyone I believed in.
—Marilyn Monroe

Drew

We sit next to each other at the round table surrounded by a crush of people, the noise from their constant chatter deafening. We say nothing to each other throughout the entire meal, for at least an hour, if not longer. I know it's stupid, but she makes me nervous and I want to get this just right.

It's like I can't find words. What can I say to follow up that kiss in the backseat of my dad's car? I don't want to cheapen the moment. I sit here and I'm wallowing in it still. Thinking like a chick, reliving the moment over and over again in my mind.

How she responded to me, the little sounds of pleasure she made in the back of her throat. The feel of her warm, velvety tongue as it slid against mine, her hands in my hair. I can't remember the last time I was kissed like that. Have I ever been kissed like that? Hell, I really don't think so.

The realization stops me cold.

We may not speak, but I'm extremely aware of her. The sound of her soft breathing, her sweet scent that makes my mouth water. The heat of her skin, the way her bare shoulder brushes against my arm when she reaches for her glass of water. I wonder if she's touching me on purpose.

Out of the corner of my eye, I watch her drink. Her full lips as they curve around the glass, the delicate line of her throat and its movement as she swallows. The impulse to kiss all that exposed skin is so strong I clench my hands into fists and rest them on my thighs. Willing myself to stop thinking like an idiot.

It doesn't work. I can't stop thinking about her. How she felt in my arms, the taste of her still on my lips. I don't ever fucking think like this, ever. I stuffed all useless emotion down deep inside me a long time ago and I've refused to let it back out. It's pointless. I'm like a robot most of the time. Going through the motions, getting through life one day at a time.

But this girl . . . she doesn't feel pointless. She's real and she's beautiful and she fits perfectly when she's in my arms. She makes me want to feel.

So dangerous to think like this. I don't mean anything to her. I'm a means to an end. A job with a paycheck. I did this to myself and now I regret it.

I scowl and slug back the beer I got from the bar earlier. It's my second one and if I have to endure this for much longer, I'm grabbing another soon. I'm pissed that my plan to parade around a fake girlfriend has gone straight to hell and I have no idea how to stop this train wreck called my emotions. I'm not even sure if I *want* to stop this.

That's the stupidest thing of all. How much I want to torture myself. But if it feels good being with her, why would I want to stop?

You've done other things that felt real good, but you knew you should stop.

I hate that voice inside my head. It reminds me of all my faults. All the bad shit I've done. I'm not a good person and I know it. I don't need the constant reminders.

"Drew, there you are!" Damn it, it's Kaylie, and she's got two friends trailing behind her. All girls I went to school with, and all of them perfectly dressed and done up so they look like identical plastic Barbie dolls. It's hard to tell them apart. "We've been looking all over for you. You remember Abby and Ella, right?"

"Yeah. Hey." I flick my chin in greeting and they all simultaneously flutter their eyelashes at me in response, giggling as they watch me. It's completely unnerving and I wish they'd leave.

Beside me, I hear a quiet snort emanate from Fable, which makes me smile. Glancing over my shoulder, I see the slightly bemused look on her face, mixed with a dose of irritation. Kaylie is persistent, I gotta give her that, but I wish she would catch a clue.

"There's dancing later, you know," Kaylie says, oblivious to the death glare Fable's throwing at her. "Maybe I could steal you away from your—girlfriend. We could catch up, since it's been a while."

She makes it sound like we used to be together or something, when truthfully I can barely remember her. I don't know why this girl is so hell-bent on pursuing me.

"Every dance is taken by me tonight. Sorry." Fable's voice is bright and cheery, but she doesn't sound one bit sorry. Plus, she's resting her hand on my upper thigh, her fingers curving around my leg so they're almost brushing against my dick. It's a possessive move and I freaking love it.

"Yeah, uh . . . sorry, Kaylie." I offer her an apologetic smile, which she doesn't bother returning. She leaves in a huff, flicking her blond hair over her shoulder as she turns and walks away with her little drones. I watch them go, ultra-aware of Fable next to me. More aware of her small hand that still rests on my thigh.

I don't want her to move it, either.

"Tell me what that girl is to you."

She sounds mad. I look at her, my gaze meeting hers. Those green eyes are shooting fire and I'm her target. "Nothing. I knew her in high school, but we hardly talked."

Fable's lips are firm, her eyes hard. She looks ready to kick some ass. "She acts like an old girlfriend."

"She wasn't." I shake my head.

"You banged her, then." Her eyes narrow into slits and my heart constricts in my chest as the realization hits.

Fable is jealous. And if the gloating sensation floating through me makes me an ass, then so be it. I'm actually getting some emotion out of this girl. She acts like she cares.

"I didn't bang her." My voice is soft. I don't want her mad. Reaching out, I touch her, drift my fingers across her cheek as I stare at her lips. I want to kiss her. Reassure her that there's nothing between Kaylie and me—no history, nothing.

"Good." Her hand drops away from my thigh and she pulls back from my touch. I'm left reaching for air and I watch in disbelief as she withdraws into herself completely.

She's shut me out in the space of about ten seconds and it's the weirdest thing I've ever seen.

I had her; now I don't. And I have no clue why.

She pushes back her chair and stands, holding out her hand toward me. "Could I have my cell, please?"

"Where are you going?" I reach inside my pocket and pull the phone out, giving it to her. I'm struck again by how gorgeous she looks in that dress. I know she'd look even more gorgeous out of it.

"Outside. I need to call my brother and make sure he's okay." She offers me a quick smile and before I can ask if she needs me to come with her, she's gone, threading through the crowd and headed toward the doors that lead outside onto a giant terrace that overlooks the golf course.

The room swallows her until I can't see her any longer, and my throat gets tight. I miss her. Ridiculous, considering that I hardly know her, and we've only been together like this for three freaking days if you count the day we drove down here, but still.

"She's not the one for you, you know."

A rough breath leaves me and I close my eyes, wishing I were anywhere but here. With *her*. Opening my eyes, I turn to see Adele sitting in Fable's just-vacated chair. The seat is still warm and I've already got Adele harassing me. I really don't need this shit. "Stay out of my life." I keep my voice low. I don't want anyone to overhear us.

"You can't avoid me forever. You know I'm going to get you alone sometime." She smiles, and her lids lower over her dark eyes. "You're using her as a shield, but I'll make it happen eventually."

"I'm not using her," I start, but Adele cuts me off with a look.

"You think I didn't miss that tentative little kissing session in the backseat of the car? Just because your dad and I were fighting doesn't mean I'm not aware of every single thing you do." Her smug smile fills me with revulsion. "I'm sorry, but whatever that was between you two looked like two beginners who have no idea what you're doing with each other. Like you've never even touched each other before. Tell me the truth. Are you really with her?"

Panic settles in and my throat is as dry as the Sahara. I don't want to answer. It's none of her goddamned business, but I know she won't let it go. She'll keep at it and keep at it until I give in. I always used to give in to Adele, and I hate that about myself.

Hate it.

I glance across the table, trying to catch my dad's eye, but he's so engrossed in conversation with the guy sitting next to him, he's not noticing anything. "We're really together," I say through clenched teeth, trying not to look at her. The disgusted sound she makes draws my attention, though, despite my efforts.

Her eyes flicker the slightest bit, revealing her hesitation, but she forges on. "So. Is she any good in bed? Does she know any special tricks?"

Jesus! I knew this would eventually happen, but not here. Not surrounded by hundreds of people. "Don't fucking go there."

Her smile widens. She knows she's struck a nerve. "Does she keep you satisfied, Andrew? That's rather difficult, you know. Once someone breaks down all those steel walls you so carefully build around yourself, you're quite . . . insatiable."

Shame washes over me and I stand so fast, my chair falls to the ground with a loud clatter. Everyone at our table looks at me, and my cheeks heat with embarrassment.

Adele sits there as serene as a queen on her throne. She doesn't bother looking at me. She knows what she's done.

"You okay, son?" my dad asks, his brows furrowed.

I don't answer him. Instead, I escape, desperate to get away from Adele. I need to get out of this crowd. The room feels like it's closing in on me, and my head is spinning. I don't know if it's from anxiety or the two beers I drank tonight.

All I know is I need fresh air. I'm headed for the terrace.

Headed for Fable.

Fable

"You're still at Wade's house, right?" I take a drag of the cigarette I bummed from someone and exhale, momentarily captivated by the thin tendrils of smoke that float in the air. It's cold as hell and I'm totally sneaking this stupid cigarette, since there are no-smoking signs all over this freaking terrace. What's the point of having an outdoor area if you're not going to let people smoke?

"Yeah, yeah, I'm still here." Owen sounds irritated as hell but I don't care. It's past nine o'clock, he should be in bed at ten, and I want to make sure he's where he's supposed to be.

"Bedtime is ten—don't forget it." I flick ashes over the railing, again with the litterbug routine and I feel like a shit. What is it about all these fancy rich people that makes me act like I grew up in a gutter?

"But that's so early. Wade doesn't go to bed till eleven." He's whining. Yet again. Reminding me that he's completely immature and still in so many ways a little boy, though he's desperate to prove he's practically a man who can take care of himself.

"Well, good for Wade. I still think you should at least be in bed by ten," I relent, knowing he probably won't listen to me.

I hate being away from him. There's something going

on, something he's hiding from me, but I can't put my finger on exactly what. I just hope he can keep his act together until I come home.

"Whatever," Owen mutters. "Most of the time you act like you're my mom, you know?"

My throat swells up and I fight off the tears. I'm totally emotional tonight and I can't really explain it. I blame Drew and his stupid, perfect lips. That kiss rattled some weird emotion inside my chest and I've been near tears ever since. "Someone has to stay on top of you."

He laughs. "Ain't that the truth?"

"Oh my God, use real words, please." I laugh, too, pleased that he's in a good mood. Earlier when I talked to him, he'd been wary and evasive. I don't want him keeping secrets from me, but I know it's natural, considering he's thirteen and all. His behavior will only get worse, too, I'm sure. But I'm prepared. At least as prepared as I can be.

Men and their deep, dark secrets. I know Drew's got a ton of them. I'm not sure what they are, but I have a feeling they're pretty major. He's all bottled up and tense. I felt it in his body when he kissed me and I was in his arms. His body rigid, as if he was holding himself back.

I didn't want him to hold back. Not then, and definitely not now. He puts up this façade for everyone and I'm starting to wonder exactly who the real Drew is. And does he even know?

"I'll call you tomorrow, okay? Be good." I draw on the cig, holding the smoke in my lungs before I release it slowly. God, I know how bad this is for me but I can't help it. Smoking relaxes me. And hanging out at this shitty country club dinner, I need as much relaxing as I can get.

" 'Bye, Fabes." No one else calls me that, just Owen. "Love you."

"Love you, too," I whisper, ending the call. I clutch the phone in a death grip since I don't have a purse and I really don't feel like shoving it in between my boobs.

"Smoking kills, you know."

Drew's deep, sexy voice washes over me and I glance over my shoulder, spotting him standing a few feet away. His hands are shoved in his pockets and the wind ruffles his dark hair.

He looks irritated and so gorgeous. I wish I could take a picture so I could capture this single breathtaking moment for all eternity and always have it—and him—with me.

"Following me?" I ask as I stub out the cigarette on the wooden railing. I don't know what to do with it, so I leave it there like the total litterbug I've become.

"I needed to get out of there."

"Me, too," I sigh. I turn my attention back to the golf course and just beyond, the ocean. I wonder if we'll come back here so I can see this view in the daylight. These rich people have no idea what sort of beauty surrounds them.

They see this every single day and it's nothing special. They probably don't even notice.

I wonder what it's like, to be that numb to such beautiful surroundings. Of course, I'm numb to the mundane that surrounds me on a daily basis. Maybe we all move through life comfortably numb. Reminds me of one of my mom's favorite songs.

"Is your brother okay?"

"He's fine." I shrug. Drew's only asking because he's being polite. Standing outside, alone in the cold night air for only a few minutes, has made this situation between us clearer. And I need that, after the mind-boggling kiss we shared.

He doesn't care about me and I don't care about him. We're doing a job and that's it. The kiss? A one-off, a way to let off steam because hey, spending all this time together in such close quarters and pretending to be a real couple is going to generate some . . . friction. Heat. Sexual chemistry.

We have it. Chemistry. I can feel it now, pinging between us, singeing my skin. I feel his eyes on me, can hear him approach, and now he's standing next to me, his arms propped against the railing just like mine. He bumps his elbow into me in a friendly gesture and I shiver. The wind is like ice and it bites at my bared skin.

"You're cold." His low murmur ripples along my nerve endings and I want to yell at him to back off.

But I don't.

"Sort of," I answer.

He chuckles. "If I had a jacket, I'd make you wear it."

I don't want him to act like a gentleman. Or like a kind, attentive boyfriend. I don't want any of these . . . lies. What I need is reality. Cold, hard facts. I need to remember the money sitting in my bank account, the fact that he's using me to push his family away. The fact that I'm using him to ensure temporary financial stability for my pitiful little family must stay prominent in my mind. I can't forget it.

"We should probably go inside," I start to stay but he touches me, settles his big hand over mine, and I shut up.

"I can't go back in there," he says, his voice so low, I almost don't hear him. "I can't face them. Not yet. Stay out here with me."

Did something happen in there that I missed? He doesn't seem too upset, but I don't know him well enough to tell. I don't answer him, figuring it's best to remain quiet and try to reassure him, and he doesn't say anything either.

But he does wrap his arm around my shoulders and haul me in close to him. I try to resist at first, stiffening my body so he can't really move me. But it's stupid to fight this, especially with the promise that he'll warm me up.

So I let go. Let him guide me into his arms, and he wraps them around me and I'm resting my hands on his hard, warm chest. His hands settle at the small of my back and I'm pressed against the railing, pressed against him. His body is hard and unyielding. He's trapped me and I have no interest in escaping.

I'm going against everything I thought and worried over only moments ago, all because he's touching me.

When it comes to Drew, I'm weak. So weak, it's almost embarrassing. But he seems just as weak over me, and I find that reassuring. At least we're in this screwed-up mess together.

"Did something happen in there?" I ask, curiosity killing me. I have to know.

"I don't want to talk about it."

I risk glancing up at him and I see how tight his jaw is. "Well, if you ever do want to talk, I'm here."

He glances down at me. There's such despair in his eyes, my chest aches for him. This perfect, beautiful boy is not so perfect after all. "You wouldn't understand."

I laugh, though I'm not mocking him and I hope he gets that. "I'd understand more than you think."

"If I told you the truth, you'd hate me." His voice is harsh, his expression pained. "*I* hate me for what I've done."

My stomach sinks into my toes. He sounds so lost and I realize he's right. Maybe I *don't* want to know. What he's saying—well, not saying—fills me with uneasiness. I'm scared.

What did he do that he hates himself so much?

CHAPTER 8

Day 3, 7:02 p.m.

> *I always want the one I can't have.*
> —Fable Maguire

Fable

He's ignored me all day, which is fine. Really. I don't mind being left alone at the guesthouse because oh my God, the last thing I want to do is hang out with that screwed-up set of parents of his. Drew took off to golf with his dad early this morning and I haven't seen him since. I have no idea if he's even come home. For all I know, they could be making happy family time at the main house while I'm stuck here alone.

Yikes, I sound bitter even in my own head! And besides, I know he's not home because I've been here all day and haven't seen them return.

Being alone has brought me back to reality, though. Again. And this is a good thing. I get too caught up with Drew when I'm with him and that's definitely not a good thing. This way, spending time by myself at this unreal house with the unreal view, I know it's all a fantasy.

I caught Adele snooping around the guesthouse earlier. Peeking in the windows, walking around the entire house. I watched her for a bit, hiding in corners, but then I started to get mad. What was she doing? Trying to spy on me? Or was she looking for Drew?

Finally, I couldn't take it anymore and threw open the door when I saw her skulking around the front. "Looking for someone?" I asked her, using the snottiest tone I could muster.

She crossed her arms in front of her, elegant as always in a pure white sweater and black leggings. I would look like a slob in a similar outfit. Of course, hers was probably designer and cost tons of money, while my sweater and leggings would come from Walmart or Target. "I thought you were gone," she said.

"Hoping I was gone, I'm sure." I don't know where I got the balls to talk to her like that, but I'd had it. The ride home the night before had been a study in torture. No one talked and the tension had been nearly unbearable. A complete turnaround from the ride to the country club, when Drew and I kissed and he had his hands all over me.

She smirked. "You don't like me very much, do you?"

"I figured the feeling was mutual." I shrugged, trying my best to look like I didn't care, but inside my stomach had churned with nerves.

"You won't last, you know. You're not his type."

I frowned. Of course I'm not his type. That's pretty freaking obvious, but I didn't figure his bitch of a stepmother would so blatantly call me out on it. "And what, exactly, is Drew's type?"

"Someone more like me." Her smile grew, as if she knew her words socked me straight in the stomach. Without another word, she turned and walked away.

Adele's answer stuck with me the rest of the day. What the hell did she mean? I didn't like it. She talks about Drew, looks at Drew, as if he belongs to her. Almost as if they're the ones in the relationship. It's freaking creepy and makes me wonder if maybe they've fooled around in the past.

So gross. And scary. Drew acts like he hates her, and that opens up another can of worms in my brain. Lots of what-ifs I don't like thinking about because they're too ugly to face. It's none of my business, I tell myself over and over again as I sit alone and wonder.

But he's brought me into this mess. He's sort of made it my business, right?

Wrong. Some things are better left alone.

Not if someone's hurting because of them.

The internal argument battles within me for the rest of the day, until I'm a total bundle of nerves while I wait anxiously for his return. Where could he be? I know golf games can take forever, but not as long as this. And I know he's with his dad because I've kept watch on the damn garage for hours and no one's returned.

Though Adele left about thirty minutes ago. That freaks me out. What if she went somewhere to meet them?

Crap. I don't know what to do.

When the door finally opens around seven thirty, I'm filled with relief. I hear Drew's footsteps echo in the tiled entryway, then see him stride by, headed down the hall while I sit in the living area. I have one of those unbelievably soft faux-fur throw blankets draped over me and I probably blend in with the couch. He doesn't notice me, doesn't bother saying a word.

I chew anxiously on my fingernail, my stomach growling since I never ate dinner. I hear him enter his bedroom and shut the door and I let out a shaky exhale. I was holding my breath and didn't even realize it.

Not two minutes later he's out of his room, entering the living area, and stopping short when he sees me. "Hey."

"Hi." I press my lips together, tell myself to breathe.

"I didn't see you when I came in." He looks amazing in a black hooded sweatshirt and khaki cargo shorts, his dark hair ruffled by the wind that seems to be constantly blowing around here. I'd bet a million dollars he has a polo shirt on underneath. Typical golf wear, though he should be wearing pastel plaid shorts and not cargoes. Not that I know anything about golf.

"I've been sitting here the entire time."

He runs his hand over his head and my fingers literally itch to do the same. I remember how silky-soft his hair is, how much he liked it when I touched him there. Does he ever really allow anyone to touch him? He tends to move through life all by himself.

That realization fills me with sadness. While I allow an endless, faceless stream of guys to touch me. I crave it because for a brief moment, I feel like someone cares about me. The feeling is always fleeting and I end up as empty as I was before. Sometimes more so.

"I didn't know where you were all day," I say to fill the silence since he's not talking.

"I'm sorry I've been gone so long." I wonder if it took a lot for him to apologize to me. I bet he doesn't have to answer to anyone most of the time.

I shrug. I need to act like what he's done doesn't bother me. "I'm not your keeper."

"Yeah, but you're my guest. I'm sure you were bored all day." He moves closer to the couch, and that's when the smell hits me.

He reeks of beer. And his eyes are kind of bloodshot,

his cheeks ruddy. I bet he's drunk. My guard goes immediately up and I shove myself into the corner of the couch when he settles down beside me. I hate the smell of beer—crazy, considering I work in a bar.

But when I smell it at La Salle's, it's different. I'm busy, I'm moving, I'm serving customers and working my tail off. In a one-on-one situation, the scent of beer reminds me of my mom and all her shitty boyfriends. How they drink constantly. Almost all of the guys she's been with have been complete alcoholics with rage issues.

Angry drunks scare the hell out of me, and Drew's a big guy with lots of pent-up issues. If he displays even a glimmer of anger toward me, I'm out of here.

"I was fine," I say. "I sat on the beach for a long time."

"Didn't you get cold? The weather wasn't the best out there today."

I shrug. "Figured I should soak it up while I'm here, right? Doubt I'll ever be somewhere as beautiful as this again."

"I'm sorry I wasn't here, Fable." His voice is soft, his expression . . . it breaks my heart. He looks so bleak, so disturbed, I wish I could say something, do something to ease his pain.

He studies me, his blue eyes dark, his head tilted to the side. I wonder what he sees. I know what I see—a confused, lonely man who won't let anyone in.

117

For whatever stupid reason, I want to be the one he lets in. Maybe I could help him, maybe I couldn't, but he needs comfort. I can tell.

Like souls find each other, you know. As corny as it sounds, I'm starting to believe we were brought together for a reason.

Drew

As usual, she's looking at me like she can see right through me, and she's making me nervous. I've stayed away from Fable all day on purpose. Everything that happened last night left me feeling like I could spiral completely out of control if I didn't get my shit together, and quick. I haven't felt that way in a long time. This is the reason why I don't come back home.

And I'm never coming back here after this visit. I don't care how much I might hurt my dad; I can't do this any longer. I can't pretend that this place, these people, don't affect me. They do. Everything fucks with my head and reminds me of what I used to be. I don't want to be that person anymore. I'm not.

There's no other choice. I have to stay away.

Looking at Fable, seeing the sympathy in her eyes, I know I should stay away from her, too. Once she really gets to know me, I could hurt her. I know I'll hurt her. I'm afraid she's this close to figuring out what my problem is. And if she doesn't, I'm afraid I'm this close to blurting it out. Once I confess, I can never take it back. Ever. It'll be out there, making both of us uncomfortable. Ruining whatever sort of relationship, friendship—whatever you want to call it—we have.

I couldn't stand the thought, so I left the house early, jumping on the chance to golf with my dad when he asked. Not only did we play a long, intense eighteen rounds with a couple of his friends, we then ended up at the golf course bar. I'm not a big drinker but I slammed back beer after beer, enjoying the buzz the alcohol gave me. My brain settled into a numb, fuzzy place where I could just forget.

We joked, we talked, my dad bragged about what a great football player I am, and that made me feel good. Dad and I don't get a lot of time together alone. Adele's always there trying to muck stuff up, or we're doing something that doesn't allow for too much one-on-one time. The lunch we had together yesterday had been uncomfortable, and I'm thankful we got past that.

Spending today with Dad was good for both of us. But I always had that nagging feeling in the back of my mind that I was ditching Fable and doing it on purpose, and the guilt lingered.

That's why I told her I was sorry.

"I caught your stepmom sniffing around outside this

119

afternoon." Fable's tone is casual, but her words are like nine little bombs dropping all over me.

Tension radiates up my spine, across my shoulders, and I stiffen. "Yeah?"

Fable nods. "I confronted her."

"What?" Shock rips through me. So does fear. What if Adele said something?

"Yeah. She didn't like it, either. Told me that we wouldn't last, that I wasn't your usual type."

I remain silent, afraid of what she might say next.

"And when I asked her what your type was, she said *she* was."

The blood is roaring in my ears, so whatever else Fable says, I can't hear it. Her lips are moving but I literally cannot hear her.

Without thought I stand and go back to my bedroom. She's calling my name; her voice is faint and I think she's following after me, but I'm not sure. I can't see—my vision is blurred—and I'm ready to boil over in shame and fear and rage.

Adele has taken it too far. Again. She always does. I want to tell Fable everything but I can't. I'm scared she'll hate me. Judge me.

Be so disgusted by me she'll leave.

We're barely halfway into this stupid trip and it's all going to shit. I don't know how to handle this anymore.

Fable

I chase after him, calling his name, but it's as if Drew can't hear me. The way his face became so completely void of emotion when I told him what Adele said was scary. He shut down right in front of me and it was the strangest thing. Like he was throwing up some sort of coping mechanism or something.

He slams his bedroom door right in my face and I open it, bursting into his room like a woman on a mission. He's standing in the middle of the room with his back to me, his head thrown back so he's staring up at the ceiling. I wish I could read his thoughts, offer him comfort, something. Anything.

But I just stand there, shifting on my feet, overcome with confusion.

"You should go," he says, his voice darkly quiet.

"Fine, I'll leave you alone." I understand when someone wants time to himself. I'm big on that most of the time anyway.

"No." He turns to look at me, his expression harsh and unyielding. "I mean you should go, as in go home. You don't need to stay here. I don't need your help any longer."

My stomach pitches and rolls and I feel like I'm going to throw up. "I don't mind staying . . ."

"I don't want you here." He cuts me off and I clamp my

lips shut. "You don't need to be around this shit, Fable. What you've had to deal with is bad enough."

I feel like I'm going to cry. He doesn't want me here. No one wants me anywhere. My mom doesn't care if I'm dead or alive. My brother would rather be hanging with his friends. I don't really have any friends besides the few I work with, and we're really more like acquaintances. Girls don't like me because they think I'm some sort of slut who wants to steal their boyfriend.

Right now, I'm all alone. No one wants me.

Holding my head up high, I sniff, fighting off the tears. "I'll go pack my bag."

I turn and leave his room and he doesn't stop me. No surprise. What did I expect? That he would chase after me and beg me not to go after all?

Of course not. My life isn't a made-for-TV movie. I don't matter to him. I need to remember that.

My room is shrouded in darkness and I flick on the overhead light, then head over to the closet where my dusty, torn duffel bag is. It's still half full; I never really unpacked for fear of something like this happening.

Guess my psychic abilities are working at full capacity at the moment.

I start stuffing the bag full of my clothes, not bothering to fold anything. I don't know how I'm supposed to leave, but I guess I could call a taxi and have them take me to the bus station. I have the money in my bank account and my debit card is on me, so I can pay for the ticket and head on home. Hopefully I won't have to hang out at the bus station for too long.

Pulling my phone out of my pocket, I glance at the screen and see Owen has texted me. Something about spending the night at Wade's again, which I tell him is fine and that I'm coming home tonight. He responds immediately:

What happened? Get fired? Did the dad come on to you?

Long story. I'll explain when I get home, I reply, then shove my phone back in the pocket of my jeans.

I feel like a failure. I can't manage to be a girlfriend right, and all I had to do was stand there and look pretty. Smile and nod and say nothing. How hard can that be?

Pissed at myself, I go into the bathroom and clear out all my toiletries, shoving them in the cosmetics bag I brought them in. I snag my razor and travel-size shampoo and conditioner out of the shower and throw them in the bag, then zip it up, satisfied with the loud noise it makes. Everything echoes in this house, what with the soaring ceilings and the tiled floors. The main house is worse, and it grates on my nerves.

Maybe I *will* be glad to get out of here. When I get on that bus, maybe I'll be able to breathe again.

I turn to leave the bathroom and find Drew standing in the doorway, much like he was last night. He's gripping the top of the door frame and leaning his body halfway through the door. His sweatshirt is riding up, taking his shirt along with it, and his shorts hang low on his hips, exposing a thin slice of his stomach. I catch a glimpse of dark hair trailing from his navel and I jerk my gaze up to meet his, embarrassed I'm checking him out when I should be thoroughly pissed at him.

"Don't go."

I stiffen my spine. This is beyond ridiculous. All the push and pull is really screwing with my brain. "I'm not in the mood to play games, Drew."

He lets go of the doorway and enters the bathroom. I back away from him, my butt hitting the edge of the counter and stopping me. I'm trembling, but not from fear. It's because he's so close, I can smell him.

Somehow the scent of beer is gone, replaced by Drew's warm, familiar smell. I can feel his body heat, the tension vibrating off him in potent waves. "I'm so sorry, Fable. I just . . . this place sucks. And I don't blame you if you want to leave, so I was giving you an out. I was trying to convince myself that's what was best, getting you out of here, but I can't do this alone. I don't want to do this alone. I'd like it if you'd stay."

"Do *what* alone, Drew? What's so bad about your parents anyway? You don't tell me anything and my mind just . . . wanders." I inhale sharply when he stops directly in front of me, so close our chests brush against each other.

Without warning, he wraps his hands around my waist and hauls me up, setting me on the edge of the bathroom counter. I let out a little squeal and he steps in between my legs. He's even closer to me now and I tip my head back, meeting his troubled gaze.

"I don't want to talk about it," he whispers. "I want to tell you, but I can't."

I touch his face and he leans into my palm, closing his eyes. I study his beautiful face and I'm consumed by the urge to kiss him. Lose myself in him.

"Keeping it all bottled up inside isn't healthy." I stroke his cheek and he opens his eyes. "You really should talk to someone." I'm trying to make him realize that I want to be the one he talks to about whatever's bothering him.

"I can't."

"All right. Whenever you're ready, I'm here." I drop my hand from his face and steady myself on the counter, and press a kiss to his cheek. I want him to know that I'll be there for him no matter what. I don't care what sort of secrets he's hiding—and I have a feeling they're pretty awful—I want to stand by him and help him.

125

He might be more trouble than he's worth, but I don't think so. This man came into my life for some reason. Just as I came into his. Maybe we're supposed to help each other cope.

Or give each other hope.

CHAPTER 9

Day 4, 1:12 p.m.

She's beautiful, and therefore to be wooed; she is
woman, and therefore to be won.
—William Shakespeare

Drew

I took Fable to lunch as a sort of thank you for putting up
with my shit. What I did to her last night was inexcusable,
but somehow she found a way to forgive me. She's so good
to me, I don't know what I did to deserve her.

Buying her a nice lunch is such a lame attempt to show
my appreciation, but it's all I've got. What I really want to
do to show my thanks, I don't think she'd be very receptive
to. The sweet kiss on the cheek she gave me last night and
the reassuring hug she offered before we both went to bed

definitely had more of a sisterly vibe than an I'm-hot-for-you vibe.

Too bad, because she's driving me crazy and I'm having a hard time concentrating. I'd rather take her to bed, strip her naked, and bury myself inside her so I can forget, for at least a little while. I want to map every inch of her skin with my mouth. I want to sit with her in my arms and kiss her for hours, until our lips are swollen and our jaws are tired. I want to know what she looks like when she comes. And I want to be the one who makes her come with my name falling from her lips.

I have never felt this way before about any girl. Ever. I sound like a complete pussy, but Fable overwhelms me—in a good way. And I've known her less than a week.

Sometimes, I guess that's all it takes.

"I love this restaurant." She looks around after the waitress brings us our plates, the smile on Fable's face the happiest I've seen her since I brought her to this town where I grew up. "It's so cute. And the food smells amazing."

Everything in downtown Carmel is what I'd label as cute. It's got a doll-like feel to it, lots of cottages everywhere and everything's tiny, all the narrow passages and secret hideaways. It's like a fairy tale.

"Dig in," I encourage because I'm starving and ready to take my own advice. I ordered a chicken club sandwich while Fable ordered some sort of Asian chicken salad. I take a couple of bites, so involved in stuffing my mouth full of food that I'm missing out on the look of pure bliss on Fable's face as she eats.

I set the sandwich on my plate, completely transfixed. It's ridiculous, my reaction to her. Doesn't help that I'm horny as hell and everything she does seems to turn me on.

But she's really enjoying that salad. Her eyes are half-closed and she's wearing this dreamy expression. She licks her lips, the sight of her pink tongue doing me in, and I swallow hard, my appetite for food suddenly gone.

My appetite for Fable comes roaring to life instead.

"This is amazing. Like, the best dressing I've ever tasted." She looks at me, her delicate brows bunched. "Are you okay? I thought you were hungry."

"Uhh . . ." Busted.

"You're not eating. You don't like it?" Her concern is sweet, but this has nothing to do with a freaking sandwich and everything to do with her. How much I want her.

And I want her pretty damn bad.

For once, I'm ready to just go with this and not worry about the consequences. We're attracted to each other. She won't have any expectations, and neither do I. My turbulent past can be pushed away and replaced—at least temporarily—with new memories I can make here with Fable.

"The sandwich is good." I take another bite to prove it,

and she smiles her approval before she starts back in on her salad.

It hits me then that we're on a lunch date. I'm the most pathetic twenty-one-year-old guy alive. I play football, I get good grades in college, I have girls dying to go out with me, and I've never really taken a girl on a date. I have no idea how to be in a relationship. My past has turned me off to all that stuff and I've let it rule me for far too long.

"Tomorrow's Thanksgiving," Fable says after she takes a drink of her iced tea. "Does your family have a big get-together or what?"

"Not really." Well, we haven't since my sister, Vanessa, died, but I'm not going there. Too heavy of a topic today. "The last few years we've gone on vacation during Thanksgiving."

"How fun." Her smile is sweet but it doesn't quite reach her eyes. She's just saying that because she thinks I expect her to. She sees how fucked-up we all are.

She's the first person who's figured that out.

"Besides, most of my dad's family is on the east coast. My dad is from New York originally," I continue.

"Really?" She wipes her mouth with a white cloth napkin, then drops it into her lap. My gaze settles on her lips. They're plump, a pretty shade of pink, and I'm dying to taste them again.

It's like I woke up this morning with sex on the brain.

Pretty accurate, considering the morning wood I was sporting. I'd dreamed of her, misty, out-of-focus images of the two of us tangled in the sheets. She's consuming me and I'm letting it happen. Reveling in it, really.

"Yeah. My mom was from there, too." I frown. I don't want to think about her either.

"Have you gone back and visited?"

"Not in years, but yeah. My grandparents live in a walkup in Brooklyn. It's a totally different way of life there." I'd like to go back. My grandma and grandpa are old and they might not be around much longer.

But they don't really like Adele, so we didn't go to see them much.

"I'd love to go there sometime." She sighs wistfully. "I've always wanted to see New York City."

"It's an experience, that's for sure." I wish I could take her. Totally presumptive of me, but I'm compelled by the need to make her happy. Show her stuff that I know her life won't allow her to see.

"Tell me something," I say when we're finished eating and waiting for the waitress to bring us the check.

"What do you want to know?" Wariness flits in her eyes and it calls to me. We're more alike than I ever thought, and I find that reassuring.

"How did you get your name?" When she frowns, I continue. "Fable. You have to admit, it's pretty unusual."

"Oh." Her cheeks turn pink, like she's embarrassed, and she drops her gaze to the table. "My mom. She's . . . different. When I was born, she took one look at me and declared me a wise soul. Supposedly she knew without hesitation I'd have many stories to tell. At least, that's what she told me when I was around five. My grandma said the same."

"A wise soul, huh?" I study her and those big, fathomless green eyes are looking right back. She does seem so much more mature than other girls I know our age. She's dealt with a lot more, too. She seems to take care of everyone. So who takes care of Fable? "Do you have a lot of stories to tell?"

She slowly shakes her head, her cheeks darkening to crimson. "My life is infinitely boring."

"I doubt that." I find her mysterious. She puts on a front, like she's tough and takes no shit, but I get the sense that there's a giant vulnerable side to her.

"If you're referring to my supposed sexual escapades, really. Totally boring. There's nothing to tell. Most of the stories floating around out there aren't true anyway." Her mouth is screwed up so tight after that statement, her lips practically disappear.

I'm momentarily taken aback by what she said. I'm trying to get to know her, not pry into her private business and her sexual past. I'm certainly not ready to go there yet.

I don't know if I ever will be. "I don't care about any of that."

"Yet it's precisely why you chose me to be your fake girlfriend." The hurt in her voice is unmistakable. By choosing her, I've hurt this already-damaged girl. The fact makes me feel like shit.

"I'm not going to lie. You're right." Reaching across the table, I take her hand in mine and entwine our fingers. Hers are slender and so very cold. I give them a squeeze in the hope I can warm them up. "But now, I'm really glad I chose you."

Her gaze meets mine once more, stark and wide, and I feel as if I just bared my soul. "I'm glad you chose me, too," she admits, her voice so soft I almost didn't hear her.

A rush of emotion burns through me and I try my best to keep it easy and light between us. But inside, I'm reeling. We make small talk and I pay the bill, yet all I can think about is her. How much I want her. How easily she's snuck into my life and how I can't imagine her out of it.

Completely crazy.

Plus, whatever happened last night eased the tension between us and we're a lot more open with each other this afternoon. So open that when we leave the café and head up the steep sidewalk toward where I parked my truck, I grab her hand and she lets me hold it.

Like we're a real couple.

"Smells like rain," Fable murmurs, and I glance up at the sky and notice the dark, swollen clouds hanging low.

"Yeah, it does." The first drop hits the moment I say the words and she smiles and laughs, the sound sliding over me, twisting me up inside. I love the sound and I want to hear her do it again.

Fat raindrops start to fall and we stop and look at each other. I tighten my hold on her hand and we start to walk faster, as if we can escape the rain as it comes down harder and harder. Until we're in the middle of a torrential downpour and we're getting soaked to the bone.

"How far did we park again?" she asks. The rain is coming down so hard, I can barely hear her.

"Way too far." I went to a public lot so I wouldn't have to worry about the parking meters, and now I wish I hadn't done that. The sidewalks are already virtually abandoned. The rain is starting to come down in sheets and we still have blocks to go.

"Maybe we should duck into a store and wait it out for a bit," she suggests.

That would work, but I see a better solution. Dragging her with me, I slip inside a narrow alleyway that I know leads to an artist's studio and gallery. The alley is completely covered overhead, thick ivy growing along the sides and across the trellis that's built there. It's dark and safe from the rain, and little white twinkle lights have been strewn among the ivy in preparation for the upcoming holiday season.

It's downright magical and I notice how Fable stares up at it in wonder, her lips parted, her eyes wide. She turns to look at me, her long blond hair sopping wet, her cheeks sprinkled with raindrops. Without thought, I reach out and wipe the droplets away with my thumb, first from one cheek, then the other. A tremble moves through her and she presses her lips together, her gaze dropping to the ground.

"Cold?" I murmur. I'm overwhelmed with the need to touch her, to keep on touching her. She's somehow become my lifeline.

Fable slowly shakes her head, then lifts her gaze to meet mine once more. "This spot, it's so pretty. Are you sure it's okay if we hide out here for a few?"

"Yeah. Definitely." I pull her in to me because I can't resist and she comes willingly, staring at my lips. We're sharing the same thoughts and that fills me with relief. She wants this as much as I do.

But she's so tiny, I tower over her, and I glance around, spotting a wooden bench that's to the right of us. I grab her by her waist, making her squeak, and I stand her on top of it so now she's the one who's taller than me.

"What are you doing?" She settles her hands on my shoulders, her fingers digging into the wet fabric of my shirt.

"Letting you take the lead," I say, hoping she will.

Damn, I want her to. So bad, it's killing me. I rest my hands on her hips, wishing she wasn't wearing jeans. Really wishing she wasn't wearing anything at all and that we were somewhere else, back at the guesthouse, her body tucked beneath mine as we explore each other with our hands and mouths.

Being with Fable frees me. I wish I had realized it sooner.

Fable

Something has changed within Drew since last night. Where before he was tense and secretive, today he seems more open and happier than I've ever seen him. Since we've come here, we've talked, we fought, we talked some more, and somehow that's brought us closer together.

But I'm also afraid. He goes back and forth. One minute open and charming and so irresistible he steals my breath, then the next he's dark and withdrawn, quiet. It takes a lot of energy to spend time with Drew but when he's acting like this, I forget all the drama and revel in just being with him.

The unexpected rainstorm has made me wet and miserable, but I don't care. Not when I have Drew staring up at me, his blue eyes locked with mine. His face is damp with raindrops and his hair is soaked, as are his clothes, just like mine. But we're in this little tunnel of an alley, covered by a wooden trellis overgrown with ivy, and it's kind of cozy. The storm has darkened the afternoon sky, and tiny white Christmas lights cast a faint glow upon us, the only sounds our accelerated breathing and the rain falling on the sidewalk and street only a few feet away.

I feel alone with him. Completely and totally isolated, not worried who might see us or what they might say. We can do whatever we want without fear of judgment or snide remarks. The jealous girls and the jealous stepmom fade away until it's just me and him and the rain.

Studying his face, I smooth my index finger along one cheekbone, then the other. He didn't shave this morning and the stubble on his face is scratchy. Makes me wonder what it would feel like to have him rub against my sensitive body parts with those roughened cheeks.

A shiver moves through me at the thought.

He's completely still, only the faint flicker of his eyelids giving away that he's affected by my touch, and becoming bolder, I trace his mouth. Slowly, along the curve of his upper lip, then the full lower lip, my finger lingering in the corners, absorbing the tiny droplets of water that dot his skin. He parts his lips, capturing the tip of my finger between them, and a gasp escapes me when he gently bites my finger, then licks it.

God! He's killing me. I don't know why he's bolder

today, I don't know why he's suddenly making moves on me, but I'm not questioning it. I want this. I want him.

"You going to kiss me or what?" he asks after I remove my finger from between his lips. "You're torturing me, you know."

"Maybe I want to." I feel flirty, mischievous, and the slow grin that spreads across his face at my remark was worth it.

Drew slides his hand up my back until he's cupping my nape, his fingers gripping my damp hair. I dip my head, our mouths brushing faintly, and it's as if a spark of electricity lights between us.

I'm instantly hungry for him, but I force myself to use restraint. I don't want to rush this moment. There's a sort of magic in this space that's woven its spell around us and I'm not ready to break it yet.

I want to make this moment with him last.

Our lips meet again and again in the most chaste of kisses; every time his mouth connects with mine, tingles dance in my stomach. My skin is covered in gooseflesh and I wind my arms around his neck, slide my fingers into his wet hair, and clutch him close. His other arm is wrapped around my waist, and he pulls me in closer until our wet bodies are plastered together.

"Fable." He whispers my name, his voice deep and sexy, and I part my lips, breathing into him. His mouth is soft and sweet, his tongue warm and damp as it tangles with mine. The slow burn deep in my belly is flaming higher. Higher still, until I'm ravenous, so hot I wish I could claw my clothes off and rub my naked body against his.

The slow kisses give way to hot, frantic ones. His fingers are so tight in my hair it hurts, but I don't care. I'm starving for him and I want more. I want everything he can give me.

He breaks the kiss first and I lean my forehead against his, our breathing out of control and loud in the otherwise hushed quiet of the tunnel. The rain seems to have lessened; it's not as loud, and I open my eyes to find him watching me carefully.

"Should we make a run for it?" he asks.

I don't know how to answer. I don't want him to let go of me. He has such a tight hold, I feel safe. Protected. "It's still raining."

"Not as hard, though."

"We'll get soaked," I point out lamely.

"We're already soaked." He kisses me, keeping his mouth close to mine when he whispers, "I want to get you out of the rain and back to the guesthouse so we can really be alone."

My heart flutters in anticipation at his words. He wants me. And I want him, too. "Okay," I agree with a nod, and he carefully lifts me off the bench, letting me go so that I slide down the length of his body the entire way. I feel everything, his hard, unyielding muscles, how much I affect him . . . it's exhilarating, how much power I have over him at this very moment.

What's about to happen will change everything between us. And for once, I'm looking forward to it. There's no shame in sex when you're with a person you care about. He isn't just another anonymous boy I'm using to ease that lonely ache inside me.

The realization both excites and terrifies me.

Drew

I couldn't drive back to the guesthouse fast enough. Traffic was shit, what with the rain, and the roads were slick. I needed to be careful; I caught my back tires skidding across the asphalt a few times when I turned corners, and I lowered my speed. Tried my best to be patient.

But with Fable sitting in the passenger seat all wet and sexy, looking good enough to eat, it was tough.

The moment we get home, I'm out of the truck and opening the door for her. The rain has eased up, though it's still steady and I have no idea if anyone's home.

Hell, I don't really care, either. I'm so eager to get Fable inside, I can hardly see straight.

She's giggling when I pull her into the guesthouse and

shut and lock the door with a finality that brings me complete satisfaction. No one's going to interrupt this. I won't allow it. I have to get Fable naked. Have. To. There's no other choice.

I press her against the wall next to the front door and brace my hands above her head, kissing her until we're both stupid with lust. Our hips connect, grinding against each other, and the wet clothes we have on are driving me crazy, so I reach for the hem of her shirt and slowly start to tug upward.

"Are you trying to strip me?" She's teasing. I love the sound of her voice, how it's full of affection, and I nod, unable to say a word for fear I'll ruin the moment.

She pushes at my chest so I have no choice but to step back, and I watch breathlessly as she reaches for her shirt and slowly lifts it up, up, until she's pulling it over her head and letting it fall from her fingers to the floor. She stands before me in a pale pink bra trimmed with black lace, her breasts plumped over the cups, and holy shit, all I want to do is take her bra off so I can touch her there.

Her eyes are glowing as she reaches for me again and I go willingly, devouring her mouth, running my hands up and down her bare sides. My fingers are getting closer and closer to her bra-covered tits and then I'm there, cupping her, smoothing my thumbs across the front of her bra, earning a sweetly agonized moan for my efforts.

I hear her whisper my name when I kiss her neck and she shivers beneath my lips. I trail my tongue along her skin, savoring her taste, the way she melts against me, and I reach behind her back, fumbling with the clasp of her bra until it comes undone.

Nerves make my hand shake and I withdraw from her, smoothing my trembling fingers over her hair, across her cheek. We stare at each other. I see how her bra straps are loose around her shoulders and I slip my fingers beneath those lacy straps and slowly pull them down, revealing her to me for the first time.

My breath catches in my throat and all I can do is stare. She's beautiful, with the prettiest pale pink nipples I've ever seen, and I touch her there, circle first one nipple with my thumb, then the other.

She closes her eyes on a hiss, her hands braced against the wall, her chest thrust forward. I lean over her and rain kisses across her collarbone, her chest, the tops of her breasts, the valley in between. I'm teasing her, teasing myself, and damn, I already feel like I'm going to explode.

When I finally take a hard nipple between my lips, she thrusts her hands into my hair, her entire body tense as I wind my tongue around and around her flesh. She's panting, I'm panting, and I wish I hadn't started this here. I should've waited until I at least got her into a bed.

"Andrew," she whispers, the sound of my full name

stopping me cold, and I go completely still as memories wash over me.

Just let me touch you, Andrew, I know you'll like it. It'll be so perfect between us. Please, Andrew. I know how to make you feel good . . .

I wrench myself out of Fable's hold and back away from her, my breath coming in ragged spurts, my brain spinning with old memories mixed with new, fresh ones.

"Drew, what's wrong? What happened?"

I focus my gaze on Fable, watch as she pushes away from the wall and comes toward me, her breasts bouncing with her every step, her expression filled with concern. I'm ruining it. I'm letting my past shade my present—hell, my entire future—and I'm filled with inexplicable rage.

This wasn't supposed to happen, not like this, not today, and I shake my head, unable to speak, my tongue feels so thick.

She reaches for me, her hand touches mine, and I yank away from her as if she'd burned me. "Drew." Her voice grows stern, reminding me again of my past, and I shake my head again, trying to shake out the shitty thoughts, but it's not working.

"Don't shut down on me, Drew. Don't run away. Tell me what's wrong." She's pleading with me, I swear I see tears streaming down her cheeks, but I can't tell her what's wrong.

If she thinks things are bad now, wait until she learns the truth.

"I—I can't do this." Without waiting for an answer, I turn away from her and escape to my room, slamming the door behind me before I turn the lock. I want her with me yet I want her far, far away. I am a total contradiction and I don't know what to do with myself anymore. Maybe I really would be better off alone.

I can't keep living my life like this, letting that—woman control me like she has, but I can't stop my reactions. I need help. I'm a fucking wreck and I need someone to save me before I become completely unsavable.

Fear ripples down my spine as I take off all my clothes, leaving them in a wet heap on the floor. I ignore my raging erection. I'm so hard my dick fucking hurts but I refuse to touch myself, no matter how much relief I'll feel when I'm done. I should be with Fable right now, not alone with my fucked-up memories.

She's banging on the door, asking me to let her in. I turn and stare at the closed door, my heart pounding so hard the sound fills my head and I can't really hear anything else. I'm breathing like I just ran hundreds of miles nonstop and my skin feels so tight, I think I might pop. I'm hot. Feverish.

My head spins.

Fuck.

Fable

I stand on my tiptoes and reach the top of the door frame, finding one of those skeleton keys that'll open any lock. Grabbing it, I jam the thin piece of metal into the lock and turn, thankful when it clicks over with ease.

Maybe I shouldn't do this. Invade Drew's privacy when he's clearly shutting me out. But the way he reacted scared me so bad, and filled me with worry, too, I knew I had to go after him and make sure everything's okay. His expression had been so full of despair when he pulled away from me, I'm not sure what set him off.

I'm scared to discover what's wrong but I have to do this. For Drew.

When I open the door, I see he's standing in the middle of the room completely naked and for a moment, I'm stunned. His body is beautiful, a masculine work of art. Broad shoulders, smooth back with fluid muscles, and a butt that looks as firm as steel. My whole body aches to feel him moving against me, with me, but I know that's not what he needs right now.

"Drew," I whisper, my voice breaking almost as much as my heart.

He whirls around, pain and humiliation written all over his face. "You should go."

"Let me help you." I start to approach him but he shakes his head.

"Go, Fable. I don't want you to see me like this." He hangs his head and my gaze drops to his lower body. He's erect, hugely erect, and I don't know what happened to ruin what was going to be an undoubtedly beautiful moment between us, but there's nothing I can do about it now.

"You can't push me away." I know that's what he's doing. What he's used to. I refuse to let him do it to me, too. I'm going to stand my ground and really help him.

I want to stick.

"You don't want me," he whispers, his voice harsh. "Not like this. I can't . . . you don't want to deal with me when I'm like this."

"Please, Drew." I'm begging and I don't care. I never do this. I don't grovel; I try my best to keep it together. But seeing him like this, he scares the hell out of me. I don't want to leave him alone and I don't want him to push me away. I feel like at this very moment, I'm all he has. "Tell me what I can do."

"You can leave." He turns away from me and I sprint toward him, grabbing his forearm and preventing him from going any farther.

"No." Our gazes clash and I stand my ground, even

though I know I must look ridiculous, half-dressed and drenched from the rain. "I'm not leaving."

His eyes drop to my still-bare chest and linger there. My nipples tighten from his blatant examination and I sway toward him as if I can't help myself. My body betrays me even though I try my best to pretend he doesn't affect me. What's happening between us isn't about sex right now. Drew needs my comfort. My acceptance.

"You're shivering," he murmurs, reaching out to grab a wet strand of hair. He rubs it between his fingers, his gaze still locked on my chest. "You need to change out of those wet clothes."

It's like he's slowly coming back to me, coming back from that dark, desolate spot where he retreated. His expression is lighter, his eyes aren't so wide and full of terror. His voice has returned to normal and he's not shaking so badly.

I'm not sure what he wants from me but whatever it is, I'm willing to give it.

Completely.

CHAPTER 10

Day 4, 9:49 p.m.

> *Love's tendrils round the heart doth twine, as round the oak doth cling the vine.*
> —Ardelia Cotton Barton

Drew

We're in my bed, Fable wrapped all around me, the two of us completely naked yet not touching in any sort of sexual way beyond being plastered together. We fell asleep like this. She's still asleep, though I've been lying here wide awake for at least an hour, my mind racing with the possibilities having her in my arms offered.

She refused to budge after I had a complete breakdown and tried my hardest to push her away. I had to admire her for that, no matter how much I didn't want her there during such a humiliating moment. Seeing me like that, all broken and dizzy and so screwed up, I must've looked like an idiot to her. At the very least, a big ol' pussy who can't handle anything sexual—shit, the rumors she could start with that knowledge alone would ruin me forever.

But she didn't bat an eyelash. Just continued to talk to me in that calm, sweet voice of hers until I had no choice but to give in. She then shoved me into bed, pulling the covers up to my chin, completely immodest without her top on, leaving me mesmerized by the sight of her bare breasts as she bent over me and pressed a kiss to my forehead.

Despite my panicking when she said my full name— that reminder of my past is still too hard to shake, I guess—I wanted her close. I wanted to feel her against me, knowing she would bring me comfort.

Torturing me, too, but I could deal with it.

So when she tried to leave, I grabbed her hand and asked her to stay. I didn't want to be alone with my thoughts and my memories. I saw the reluctance in her gaze but she stayed anyway, shedding her wet clothes completely, the sight of her beautiful slender body in all its naked glory leaving my mouth dry.

She climbed into my bed and I pulled her close. Held her to me, her back to my front, as we fell asleep to the sound of the rain falling outside. I couldn't remember the last time I felt so content, having this warm, beautiful girl so close in my arms, skin on skin, our breathing in sync, my hands resting on her soft belly.

Waking up flat on my back with her sprawled all over me, her fragrant, still-damp hair in my face, I thought I was dreaming, she felt that good. But then I realized it was all too real, and I didn't move for fear of disturbing her and causing her to leave me.

At this very moment, I don't want her away from me ever.

Carefully I run my fingers through her hair, smoothing it out, holding my breath. She snuggles closer, her face pressed against my chest, her lips brushing my skin, making me instantly hard. The rain is still falling outside; the room is completely shrouded in darkness and I can see nothing. Only feel.

I haven't felt anything in years.

She wakes slowly—I know the moment it happens, from how her breathing changes, the way she starts to withdraw from me. I clamp my arms around her and hold her close, not saying a word for fear I'll fuck up and blurt out something stupid.

Instead of trying to pull away, she lifts her head and nuzzles closer, her mouth against my neck. She kisses me there, slowly, softly, and tingles wash over my entire body at the sensation, making me shiver. I swear I feel her smile and I wrap my arm tight around her waist, splaying my fingers wide so I can touch as much bare skin as possible.

I don't know exactly what I'm doing or what I'm trying to accomplish, but I know that I can handle this. In the dark, with Fable. No memories haunting me, completely in this moment. Fable in my arms, her long hair brushing against my skin, her warm breath in my ear. She sinks her teeth into the tender flesh of my earlobe and I flinch, a huff of breath escaping me that sounds suspiciously like laughter.

"Ticklish?" she whispers and I nod, still scared to say anything, savoring the sound of her sweet, sweet voice washing over me. I've never laughed during sex before. It's never something I considered particularly funny. More like a means to an end . . .

Or a shameful, guilt-ridden secret.

"You have the most beautiful body I've ever seen," she whispers as she slides over so she's completely on top of me. The thick comforter is still covering our bodies, and her warmth seeps into mine, cocooning us in our own little private haven.

"You can't even see me." I'm surprised at how good her compliment makes me feel.

"Oh, I saw you. And I can feel you." Her hands are everywhere, searching me. Arousing me. "You're all muscle,

Drew Callahan. There's not an ounce of fat on you." I can hear the amusement in her voice and I know she's enjoying teasing me.

"That's probably not true." I choke on the last word when she slides her naked body down, then off me so she's lying on her side right next to me. She trails her hand down my chest, along my abs, her fingers gently gliding over my stomach, making it tremble. I am rock hard and aching with it and I refuse to ask her for anything more than she's willing to give.

I'm scared. Fucking scared to have sex for fear I'll ruin everything and flip out again. Have all those memories come tumbling down on me and I won't be able to deal.

What's happened to me in my past has shaded my entire life. Ruined it. I'm tired of letting it rule me.

So. Fucking. Tired.

Her hand skitters away from my cock and I breathe a sigh of relief—and agony. I'd give anything to have her hands on me. Feeling the overwhelming need to connect with her, I cup her cheek with my palm and tilt her head up, kissing her fiercely. No gentle, sweet kisses this time. I devour her, drink from her lips, suck on her tongue, and she does the same. Our hands are everywhere, mapping each other's bodies, moving into more intimate territory with every stroke of our fingers, and then I feel her tentative grip on me. Her hand is shaking and my entire body is shaking.

I groan at the sensation of her touching me like this for the first time and it emboldens her. She squeezes my dick and starts to stroke, those little fingers working me quickly into a frenzied mass of need. I kiss her again, losing myself in her taste, in her hand, and already I can feel sensations barreling down on me.

She whispers my name against my lips, her busy hand getting busier, and I groan, arching my hips into her touch. The war begins within me as I near my orgasm and I fight against it.

This isn't right. You should be ashamed. Sick to your stomach at what you're doing. You're disgusting.

I push the nagging voice in my head aside and remind myself this is Fable. Beautiful, sweet, strong Fable. That what we're doing, what we're sharing, isn't full of shame. There's nothing wrong with two people wanting to bring themselves closer together by giving each other pleasure.

It's hard, though, for me to believe it fully.

Her hand pauses and she breaks away from our kiss. "Are you okay?"

That she would even ask blows my mind. And also makes me feel like a damn wimp. I start to pull away and her grip tightens on my dick, freaking me out a little. I'm not going anywhere with that death grip on my most private parts.

"Drew. I just . . . I have a feeling this isn't easy for you. Being intimate." She sounds hesitant, unsure, and she relaxes her hold, her thumb drawing circles on the very tip of me, over and over again.

I'm going to explode. Quick. I reach for her, cupping her head with my hands as I kiss her gently, reverently.

I don't want this moment to end. And I don't want to let her in close. She's already so deep in with me, I'm afraid that if she knew what I keep hidden inside, I wouldn't be what she wanted. That I wouldn't be the man she's looking for.

"I want this," I tell her when I finally break the kiss. Her hand has dropped away from my erection but I still feel her. Want her. Need her to take me to the next level, where I can completely forget, if only for a little while. "I want this with you, Fable."

I say her name to ground me. To remind me this is happening with Fable. The girl who's become my life source in a laughingly short amount of time. The girl I'm falling for.

Fable

Drew is so huge and hard he must be in pain. That's part of the reason I touched him. I couldn't resist. Well, that and I had to know what would happen if I did. Would he push me away this time? I want to bring him pleasure because his joy is slowly becoming mine and if I can help him push out of whatever horrible thing sex makes him feel, then it's worth it.

I wish the lights were on so I could see him, but I have a feeling he's not ready for that yet.

I ache so much between my legs that I feel like I could almost die from wanting him. I wish I could take him inside me, but . . . I don't want to push. That I'm the aggressor here is sort of blowing me away, but he has awful secrets I hope I can coax out of him someday, no matter how much the idea terrifies me.

And the idea really, really terrifies me.

Drew whispers my name and I kiss him. Stroke him, grip him harder, move my hand faster. If I only give him a hand job tonight, then so be it. I sort of like the idea of us doing something so . . . juvenile. We're two adults, naked in a bed all alone in a giant house, and we could fuck each other wherever we want. He could have me in every single room in this house, out on the deck, wherever, and I'd let him, I want him that badly.

Yet here we are like we're in the backseat of a car parked in the back of the lot at the movie theater, trying to get each other off before our midnight curfew.

A low groan escapes him and he stiffens, his entire body tense for that one hanging moment before he completely falls apart. He's coming all over my fingers as I keep my hand on him, his body convulsing, his hips jerking. A potent wave of satisfaction washes over me and I lean up and kiss him, tangle our tongues together, smiling when he breaks the kiss to release a shuddery little moan.

Pulling away from him, I climb out of bed without a word and head for the bathroom across the hall. I flick on the lights, my image in the mirror startling me, and I stop and stare for a moment.

My eyes sparkle, my cheeks are flushed, and my lips are swollen from his crushing kisses. My entire body is covered in a rosy blush and my nipples are hard.

I wish Drew could see me. That we didn't have to be so covered in darkness. Does the darkness make it easier for him?

Pushing the gloomy thoughts from my head, I wash my hands, turn off the faucet, and try my damnedest to smooth out my hair. It's a tangled mess, wild waves all around my face, and I blame the rain.

I also blame the man who buried his hands in my hair so he could hold me still and kiss me senseless.

I catch his silhouette when I slip into the bedroom. He's still lying where I left him, though at least his breathing has evened out. I go to him, crawling on top of the bed, where I kneel beside him.

"Fable . . ." he starts but I shush him, leaning over his face so I can place a finger to his lips.

"Don't say a word. You might ruin it," I murmur, and I feel his faint smile against my finger.

Satisfied he's not going to say something that'll spoil the moment, I lie down beside him and pull the covers back over us. Despite my vibrating, on-edge body, I'm exhausted, and the idea of falling back asleep cradled in Drew's strong arms is just too hard to resist. I snuggle in close, resting my cheek against his rock-hard chest, where I can feel his wildly beating heart.

His fingers are back in my hair and his mouth brushes against my forehead. Contentedness washes over me, heady and potent, and I close my eyes, letting my fingers drift across his skin.

"I know tomorrow's Thanksgiving and all, so I should probably save this confession for then. But there's no way in hell I'm going to say this in front of my parents, so I'll tell you now what I'm most thankful for," he whispers against my hair, his low, deep voice soothing me, lulling me into a false hope I'm too tired to fight.

I open my eyes, staring unseeingly into the dark. "What are you most thankful for?" I ask, my breath lodged in my throat. I both want to know and dread knowing what he's about to say.

157

He's silent for a moment, as if gathering up the courage, and my heart constricts for him. "You. Being here, spending time with you, how you take care of me no matter how hard I try to push you away." His voice hitches and he clears his throat. "I'm thankful for you."

I say nothing and thankfully, neither does he for long, too-quiet minutes. My throat is clogged with some unknown emotion I can't quite put my finger on and I try to swallow past it, but it's no use. His muscular arms are tight around me, I feel like I can't move, I can't breathe, and with a little cry I slide down and slip out of his embrace, falling out of the bed when I do so.

As I scramble to my feet I hear him sit up, the blankets rustling with his movements. "Fable, what's wrong?"

Now I'm the one who's panicking and I hate it. I feel terrible. He didn't ask for this sort of crappy treatment. He's just laid his heart out and said he's thankful for *me,* and here I go trying to escape. Scared of what he's saying and how wonderfully real it feels.

But it's not real. He's caught up, just like I'm caught up, and I can't differentiate what's real from what's fake anymore. I know he's in the same place. He wants us to be real and it's easy to think we'll work together when we're all alone, pretending to be something we're not.

When we return to the real world, we'll see how different we are. How we could never be a couple.

I'm not good enough for the likes of Andrew D. Callahan.

"I—I need to take a shower." I suddenly do. The idea of scalding-hot water washing away all of my tumultuous emotions has massive appeal, and I need to get out of here.

"All right." He clears his throat, and I wonder if he realizes how uncomfortable I am. He must. "Will you . . . will you come back to bed with me when you're done?"

It took everything out of him to say that, I could tell, just by the tone of his voice. "Sure," I lie, feeling terrible. I am the worst sort of person, lying to him. I hate liars. But I'm only lying to myself by thinking Drew can somehow, some way, feel something for me.

I escape his room and hide away in the bathroom, taking the hottest shower I can stand. I scrub at my skin until it's red and raw, the steam billowing within the small room and the hot air making me dizzy. Tears are streaming down my face as I cry ugly, soundless sobs that wrack my body. I don't understand why I'm so sad or why I need to get away from Drew. I don't regret what I did for him, how I touched him and brought him relief. Release. If my touching him helped him erase even a little bit of what haunts him, I'm happy I could do that. It's the least he deserves.

But my reaction to all of this is off-the-charts ridiculous. I'm falling apart. I don't want to become dependent on Drew, yet it's too late. I am. Slowly but surely I am, and if I don't stop it soon, my heart will become so entwined with his, I know I will literally bleed if we're ever separated.

A shuddering breath escapes me as I step out of the shower and hurriedly dry myself off. I sneak back into my bedroom and slip on an old pair of sweats and a T-shirt, then dive beneath my cold-as-ice sheets and pull the covers over me, my still-hot body shivering from the difference in temperature compared to the chill in the room.

I'm totally exhausted and emotionally drained, but I don't sleep well for the rest of the night, tossing and turning, thinking of Drew all alone in the next room. I abandoned him. I let him down.

I'm no better than my mother.

With that realization, I cry.

CHAPTER 11

Day 5 (Thanksgiving), 12:55 p.m.

The more I push you away, the more I want you to push back.
—Drew Callahan

Fable

"Mom's not making Thanksgiving dinner?" I ask incredulously, fighting the urge to rush outside and inhale a cigarette. My nerves are frazzled and my hands are literally shaking, but I only have two cigs left in my secret pack. The one that was full when I arrived here. I need to save them.

"Nope. She told me there was a frozen turkey dinner in the freezer from Marie Callender's if I wanted that. Otherwise, I'm on my own." Owen sounds disgusted and I don't blame him. "I guess she went out of town with Larry. He has a daughter or something and they were going to have turkey dinner there."

Unbelievable, that Mom wouldn't bother taking Owen with her. He's her *son*. Guilt eats at me for not being with Owen, but what else is new? I'm starting to think all the money in the world isn't worth this turmoil. My heart is in tatters, my brain is sluggish, and my brother has been virtually abandoned on a holiday that our mother usually loves and goes overboard in celebrating.

Even though it's only been the three of us for so long, since my grandparents died within months of each other when I was eleven, my mom always makes a huge Thanksgiving dinner and invites everyone she can think of. Sometimes she'll have her current boyfriend in attendance; other times, friends from the bar where she likes to hang out, the lonely stragglers who have no family to spend the day with.

My mom may have her faults—and she has a shit ton of them—but she always brings in the strays for the holidays. Doesn't like to see someone hurt and lonely.

Frowning, I shake my head. Yet she'll abandon her own son. Never contact her own daughter. Sometimes I think she cares more about the people she drinks with than the people she created.

"I wish I were there." I lower my voice since I'm in the

main house, and who knows if there are spies lurking about. I wouldn't doubt it. "You shouldn't have to spend the holiday alone."

"I'll be all right." His false bravado kills me. Owen tries to act so tough all the time. I wonder if it's as exhausting for him as it is for me. "Wade's mom invited me over. I think I'll go to their house in an hour or so. Wade said they like to eat around three. Supposedly his mom makes a fucking awesome pumpkin pie."

"Don't curse." My heart lightens and I plan on sending a thank-you card, gift, whatever I can muster to Wade's mom when I get back home. "I'm so glad you have somewhere to go."

"Same here." He pauses for a moment before he says in a small voice, "I miss you."

I swallow past the lump in my throat. "I miss you, too. But I'll be home Saturday night, I promise. Let's do something Sunday, okay? Maybe we could go to the movies." We never go, it's too damn expensive, even the matinee, but screw it. We need to infuse some fun in our lives. It's too damn dreary in the Maguire household and we'll both need the escape by the time I get home.

"I'd like that, Fabes. I love you. Happy Thanksgiving."

"I love you, too. Happy Thanksgiving, sweetie." I hit END on my phone and turn to find Adele standing not five

163

feet away from me, her perfectly arched eyebrows lifted so high I'm afraid they'll fly right off her too-pretty, too-smug face.

"Well. Don't you sound cozy, chirping into your phone how much you miss and love him?" She takes a step toward me and I back away, fear shivering down my spine, though I don't know exactly why. I shouldn't be scared of this woman, despite her menacing expression and those cold, calculating eyes. She means nothing to me.

But I don't want to make waves. It's Thanksgiving, for the love of God! Getting in some sort of stupid argument with his stepmom will only hurt and humiliate Drew and I don't want to be that type of girlfriend, fake or not.

"Isn't it rude to spy on other people's conversations?" I ask, because I can't help myself. I'm pissed she's listening in, even more so that she believes I'm talking to another boyfriend, lover, whatever. I shouldn't have to explain myself. It's none of her damn business.

"Not when the conversations are happening inside my house, in my study. And when you just so happen to be the little tramp who's fucking my Andrew."

I flinch at the venom in her words. At how easily she drops the f-bomb and possessively calls him "my Andrew." "He's not yours," I whisper. *He's mine.*

I don't have the guts to say it.

Her smile is catty. "That's where you're wrong. You're

temporary. A novelty. He brought you home to shock us, to horrify us into believing he might actually want to be with someone like you, but I know the truth."

Glancing about the cavernous room, I search for an escape, but the only way I'm leaving is if I walk past her, and I don't want to. She knows it. The bitch has me trapped. "Shouldn't you be basting a turkey or something?"

Adele laughs, but the sound is brittle. And there's no humor in it whatsoever. "Trying to distract me? It won't work." She crosses her arms in front of her chest. "This holiday, it's a very difficult time for my family, you know. The two-year anniversary of my daughter's death is this Saturday."

Shock courses through me at her words. I'm literally stunned. I can't believe Drew never told me he had a sister and that she died. Maybe his problems stem from her death? But that makes no sense, not from what I've witnessed in his behavior.

"I'm so sorry," I say automatically, and I mean it. The death of a family member is awful and I wouldn't wish it on anyone, even this rude witch of a woman. I was traumatized when I lost my grandparents. They were the one constant in my world when I was young, since I couldn't count on my mother, then or now.

"Vanessa would be five now. Going to kindergarten, drawing turkeys she traced around her hand on a piece of paper." Adele's voice grows distant, as does her gaze. The sadness emanating from her is palpable, and I feel sorry for her despite how terribly she treated me only moments ago. "She was beautiful. Looked just like her father."

Drew's sister died when she was three—how? What happened? And right after Thanksgiving? No wonder he didn't want to come back here for the holiday. It's probably a painful memory he'd rather forget. And there's such an age difference between them. He would've been what, sixteen, seventeen when she was born? I wonder what took his dad and Adele so long to decide to finally have a child together. "I'm sure she was gorgeous. Your husband is a very handsome man." I don't know what else to say, and it sounds so incredibly trite I immediately regret it. Especially when she shoots me such an odd look.

"My husband . . ." Adele's voice trails off and she shakes her head. "You're right. Andy is very handsome. As is Andrew."

She always calls him Andrew. And last night, when I called him Andrew, he didn't like it. At all. He flipped the hell out, actually.

Was that the trigger? Is *she* the trigger?

"The Thanksgiving meal will be served in thirty minutes," she says crisply, all signs of mourning and sadness gone. "Afterwards, I suggest you go back to the guesthouse and pack your bags. I'll have a taxi come pick you up and take you to the bus station later this evening."

My mouth drops open in shock. She can't be serious.

"Oh yes, I have plans, little Fable. Plans that don't include you, since they involve a private family matter and you're nothing but an intruder. It's best that you leave. I already spoke to Andrew and he's in complete agreement with me." Without another word, she turns on her very thin, very high heel and walks out of the room, leaving me to slump backward into an overstuffed chair as if my legs can't hold me up any longer.

She spoke with Drew already and he agrees that I should leave tonight? This makes absolutely no sense. I don't understand what's going on and my mind is awhirl with all the information Adele just gave me.

He had a sister who died at only three years old. What happened? How did she die? Was it a sickness, a disease that took her, or did an accident happen? I can't be so completely insensitive to just point-blank ask, so I guess I'll never know unless he decides to tell me.

And since he hasn't told me so far, I'm not counting on ever knowing.

Stupid to admit, but it hurts that Drew never told me about his sister. That's a major traumatic experience and he withheld it from me. Of course, he withholds a lot of things. He's so full of secrets, I still don't feel like I know him. Not really.

Earlier this morning he was out of the house by the time I finally came out of my bedroom, but I planned it that way. Locking myself up in my room, trying like crazy to get a hold of my mom though she never returned my calls—what else is new? Then I tried calling and texting Owen, but I figured he was sleeping in and I'd been right.

In fact, I still haven't seen Drew. Is he mad at me for not coming back to his bed? Probably. It's for the best, though. Whatever this is between us, it's not happening. Not really.

No matter how badly I want it to.

Drew

"There's another man in your supposed girlfriend's life."

I turn at the sound of Adele's voice and discover she's followed me out to the garden that's connected to the backyard to talk with me. And we're all alone.

Uneasiness washes over me and I tense my shoulders, prepared to do battle. "What are you talking about?"

Adele shrugs, the look on her face unreadable. "I heard a phone conversation she was having. She told whomever she was talking to that she missed him, she wished that she were spending Thanksgiving with him, and she's planning a movie date for the two of them when she returns home."

She's totally getting off on giving me this bad news, and I'm trying my best to pretend everything's fine. That her vicious, shitty words don't affect me.

But they do. Fable withdrew from me so completely last night after what happened between us. The tables were turned and I didn't like it. She never came back to my bed. She jerked me off and left me there, adrenaline still buzzing in my veins and amping me up, making me eager to explore her body just as thoroughly as she'd explored mine.

She left me high and dry instead. I finally fell asleep when I realized she wasn't coming back, and I still haven't seen her or talked to her this morning.

It's like she's hiding away from me.

"Fable doesn't have anyone else in her life. Only me," I mumble, starting for the open doorway that leads back into the house.

Adele dodges left, grabbing hold of my arm before I can escape, her fingers digging into my flesh. "You don't know that for sure, you idiot. I'm positive that whore is out spreading her legs for anyone who asks."

I almost slap Adele across her bitchy face, I'm so angry. "Don't ever call her that," I say through clenched teeth. "Ever."

"I heard her. She called him 'sweetie.' She told him she loved him before she hung up. Face facts, Andrew. She's cheating on you with another man." Adele mock frowns at me, batting her eyelashes. "What's wrong? Do you not keep her satisfied enough? I know you like to control all of those animal urges of yours to the best of your ability but sometimes, a girl likes it when you unleash all over her."

"Fuck you. Leave me the fuck alone and stop talking shit about my girlfriend." I jerk out of Adele's hold and push past her, hurrying into the house. I need to find Fable. I need confirmation once and for all that she's not talking to some other guy while she's here with me.

I know I don't have exclusive rights to her. But the least she can do is take calls from other guys out of earshot of anyone. I mean, come on. She's making me look like a jackass and giving Adele way too much ammunition.

And the idea Fable might really be with another guy on the side while she spends time here with me? Fuck, I can't stand it!

My blood boiling and jealousy eating at me so hard and fast I'm turning into a complete dick, I stride through the house, ignoring Dad when he calls my name, ignoring Adele when she finally bursts into the house and makes a grab for me yet again. I can't find Fable anywhere inside, and when I finally do spot her standing in the front yard puffing away on a cigarette I instantly see red.

Instantly, I-want-to-kick-some-ass, bloody-as-hell red.

Opening the front door, I stalk outside, heading straight

for her. Our gazes clash and I see the fear, the wariness, the . . . matching anger in her eyes as well. She takes a long drag on her cigarette, blowing the smoke directly in my face when I stop in front of her, and I'm furious. With her. With Adele. With my dad.

With myself for thinking I could have something with this girl who clearly doesn't give a shit about me.

"You're with someone else," I say, not bothering to hold back.

She purses her lips, the cigarette dangling from her fingers. "Talking to your stepmom, I see."

"Tell me what's going on."

"How is it any of your business?" She flicks the cigarette onto the grass and grinds the heel of her boot to put it out, digging a hole in my parents' otherwise pristine lawn. My dad is going to shit a brick when he sees that.

"I've paid you a fuck ton of money to pretend to be my girlfriend this week. I think that makes it my business." I grab her arm and haul her in close, staring directly into her blazing green eyes. I want to see if she's lying to me. If everything we shared yesterday was nothing but a bunch of meaningless bullshit for her.

That thought hurts. More than I care to admit.

"So we're back to that, huh? All those sweet words and yesterday's romance evaporates after I get you off. Now we're at square one and the paid-girlfriend bit."

171

She's mad. But I'm madder. "Tell me the truth. Is there another guy?"

"Only if you tell me how your sister died," she throws back at me.

Surprise renders me silent and I let go of her, back up a few steps. *Fuck.* I hadn't counted on that. Figured I still had a little bit of time before I had to confess about Vanessa. "There's nothing to tell," I murmur, not about to go into the details, ignoring the guilt that has a death squeeze on my chest.

"Right, you just so happen to forget to mention you have a three-year-old sister who died here almost two years ago to the day. I mean, no wonder you don't want to come back to this place, Drew. I wouldn't want to either. I'm sure your house is chock-full of horrendous memories you don't want to face."

"You're damn right." She's distracting me and I'm getting angrier because of it. We are *not* going to discuss my sister any further. "Who's the guy, Fable?"

She shakes her head. "No one."

"Who's. The. Guy?" I bite each word out, so freaking tired of her bullshit.

"What? Are you jealous?"

"Fuck yes, I am!" I roar, unable to stop the words from spilling out. "After everything we've shared, especially after yesterday, you have the nerve to ask if I'm jealous? Of course, I am. This isn't a game to me, Fable. This is my life. And I want you to be a part of it. But if you'd rather fuck around with other guys, then I can't deal with that. I want you and you only. I'm not sharing you with anyone else."

My breathing's ragged by the time I'm finished with my speech and I can't believe what I just said to her. She's staring at me as if I'm crazy and maybe I am, but I can't hold back with her. For whatever reason, she makes me want to confess everything.

Every fucking thing, the good and the bad.

"Me and you, we're pretending," she whispers. There are tears in her eyes and one slips down her cheek. I want to stop it with my thumb, I want to kiss the tear away, but I don't. I can't, not after what she's said. "This isn't real. You're getting caught up in nothing."

"That's not true," I start but she shuts me up, pressing her fingers against my mouth for the briefest moment before she drops her hand.

"It is. You don't want me, not really. I'm not who you think I am. And you're definitely not who I think you are. There are so many secrets and problems between us, I think our life would be one fucked-up mess after another if we were to really try and be together. And that's never going to happen, you know this."

I can't say anything. I know she's right, no matter how

badly I don't want her to be. I'm wishing on nothing right now. And my heart is breaking for it.

"Two more days, Drew." She pauses, chewing on her lower lip. "Unless you want me to leave tonight like Adele said. She has something planned, about the anniversary of your sister's death. And clearly I'm not invited."

"I don't want you to leave," I say automatically. "Two more days—I need that from you."

"Fine." She nods once, her lips thin, her eyes imploring.

She wants to say something more, I can tell, but Adele throws open the front door, announcing, "Dinner's ready!" all cheery-like, and it's such bullshit I throw her a hard stare over my shoulder, earning a slammed door for my efforts.

"We should go in," Fable says, wrapping her arms around herself as she starts for the front door.

I follow her, realizing only later that I never found out if there really was another guy or not.

CHAPTER 12

Day 6 (Black Friday), 8:00 a.m.

> *What lies behind us and what lies before us are tiny matters compared to what lies within us.*
> —Ralph Waldo Emerson

Drew

Yesterday's Thanksgiving dinner was a disaster, not that I expected it to be anything less. Dad invited a few business associates, and while they talked Wall Street and the state of the economy at one end of the table, we were pretty much silent at the other end. Fable sat across from me, stubbornly quiet as she picked at her plate full of catered food.

Adele doesn't cook and she sure as hell wasn't going to prepare a Thanksgiving meal. I don't know if I've ever had a home-cooked turkey since the last time we spent the holidays with my grandparents in New York, and that was years ago.

The hostility in the house was off the charts. Adele tried her damnedest to talk to me but I refused. The taxi had shown up to cart Fable away just as promised later that evening and I sent the guy away, shoving two twenties in his hand as payment for his trouble.

Not once did Fable speak to me. The moment she could make her escape, she was gone, heading back to the guest-house without a good night to anyone and locking herself away in her room. She didn't come out for the rest of the night.

So I did the same, pissed at myself that I let her get under my skin. I didn't sleep much, hadn't really slept much the night before either, and now I'm lurking outside Fable's closed door, tempted to bust in there and make her talk to me.

This is definitely not like me. I'm not confrontational. I hate facing my feelings. But damn it, that fight between us yesterday left me raw and hurting. I feel like a pussy for even thinking this, but I thought what we had was turning into something special.

Guess I was wrong.

But see, this is where my stubbornness kicks in for once in my personal life. I don't want to be wrong. I don't think I *am* wrong. For whatever reason, she's running scared.

I can't blame her. I do the same damn thing, day in and day out. The only time I feel completely in control of my life is out on the football field. Being trapped here for the last few days, I'm jonesing to get back to it. Get my head out of the bullshit and back into the game.

Go back into unfeeling robot mode and forget everything else.

Irritated with myself, I knock on her door and turn the knob, surprised to find it unlocked. I don't bother giving her even a second to respond—I stride into her dark room, stopping at the foot of the bed to find her a sleeping, dead-to-the-world lump in the center of the mattress.

Her blond hair is strewn about the pillow in tangled waves, her face soft with sleep. Rosebud lips parted, the covers are pushed down to her waist and she's wearing a skimpy pale-blue tank top with no bra, her nipples clearly visible beneath the thin fabric.

The thin top, her hard nipples beneath—I'm captivated, salivating really. It's cold as hell in the room and I go to her, grabbing the edge of the comforter so I can pull it up over her body. My knuckles brush against her chest—I did it on purpose, I'm not going to lie—and her eyes fly open at first contact. She sits up so fast she nearly nails me in the jaw with her forehead, and I take a quick step back, saving myself from massive injury.

"What are you doing?" She pulls the covers up to her

chin, covering up all that pretty exposed skin, and disappointment crashes into me. "Sneaking around my room?"

"I wanted to make sure you were okay." Lame-as-hell answer, but it's all I got.

"What time is it?" She leans over and grabs her phone off the bedside table, checking the clock with an aggravated groan. "Why would you think something's wrong with me this early in the morning?"

"You locked yourself up in here over twelve hours ago. For all I know you could be unconscious. How was I supposed to know?" I feel defensive. Her reaction makes me defensive, and I don't know how we skipped backward and ended up hostile toward each other again. I fucking hate it.

I want the new Fable back. I want the new *us* back.

There was never any "us," you asshole.

Clamping my lips shut, I sit on the edge of the bed, sad when she skitters away from me as if she needs the space. I've had this idea lurking in the back of my mind since about three this morning and I hope it's going to heal what damage has been done to our tentative relationship. If she doesn't agree . . .

I don't know what else to do.

"Well, I'm fine," she retorts, setting her phone down, her gaze locked on her bent knees in front of her. "You can leave now."

"I was hoping I could ask you to go with me some-where."

She flicks her head in an I-don't-give-a-shit way. "I don't know if we should hang out together anymore, Drew. I know we're supposed to be pretending we're boyfriend and girlfriend, but this week is almost over and I don't think we need to make a big show of it."

Fuck, what did I do? I have no idea, and she's not going to tell me unless I drag it out of her. "I wanted you to come with me to the cemetery. I need to visit my sister's grave."

Her gaze finally meets mine, those green eyes full of pain and sympathy. All for me. "I don't know if I should . . ."

"I want you there." Reaching out, I grab her hand and cradle it in mine. Her fingers are ice cold and she tries to withdraw, but I tighten my grip. "I need you there, Fable."

"I thought Adele had something planned for family only." She lifts her chin, looking defiant. Vulnerable. Beau-tiful.

So beautiful I'm tempted to haul her into my arms and never let her go. But I don't.

"I'm not going with them." It would be my every night-mare come to life. Adele a weeping, emotional wreck and me expected to stand by her, full of sympathy and offering her hugs.

I can hardly stand the thought of her touching me, let alone actually letting her.

Fable is quiet. I can tell she's considering my request, which fills me with relief. I don't want to go alone, I don't want to go with my parents either, but I need to go and pay my respects to my baby sister. The idea of going alone fills me with such overwhelming sadness, I know I'd fall apart the second I parked my truck in the cemetery lot. I wouldn't be able to go in there, and I need to.

Having Fable by my side will give me the strength I freaking need to visit my sister's grave. Beg her forgiveness at her gravestone for not taking care of her and hope like hell when I tell Fable the truth, she won't hate me for what I've done.

And maybe, just maybe, her acceptance will help ease the hatred I feel for myself.

"I'll go with you," she says, her voice low, her gaze downcast once more. "When do you want to leave?"

"I need to take a shower. I'm sure you do, too." When she nods, I continue. "A couple of hours, then? By ten?"

"That sounds good." She nods again and slowly releases her hold on my hand, her fingers drifting along the length of mine. Chills steal over me at the subtle contact and when I look at her, she's watching me, her lips parted, her eyes wide. So fucking beautiful in her tousled, still-sleepy state, it hurts to stare at her for too long.

"Thank you," I whisper. "For saying you'll come with me."

"Thank you for trusting me enough to ask." She licks her lips, leaving a damp sheen on them, and I want to kiss her so bad, I ache with it. "That's why I was so mad, Drew. After what happened yesterday, what you and Adele accused me of, it felt like you didn't trust me. And all I've ever been is honest with you."

She's right. I know this. I overreacted. Adele pushed all my buttons and I fell for her tricks. So stupid.

"I shouldn't have listened to Adele." I take a deep breath and let it out. "I'm sorry."

A little smile curls her lips and my heart flutters. "You're forgiven. And just so you know. The guy I was talking to yesterday?"

Now my heart is pounding. "Yeah?"

"It was Owen. My brother."

I feel one hundred times the jackass. Of course she was talking to her brother. She's worried sick about him most of the time. "I should never listen to Adele."

"No, you shouldn't."

"I feel like an asshole."

"Yesterday, you sort of were one." I'm about to say something, but she cuts me off. "Truthfully? I liked seeing all the anger. It means you actually feel something, you know?"

I'm quiet. She's right. I can't remember the last time I went off like that. Do I ever go off like that? A fuse had been lit within me and I was unable to contain it.

"I'm going to take a shower." She flicks her chin at me. "You should go. I don't want you to see me. My shirt's practically see-through."

"Fable, I hate to break this to you, but I've already seen you," I remind her, my voice low.

Now it's her turn to remain quiet and with a grin, I stand, heading for the door. "I liked what I saw, too," I call over my shoulder.

Her soft laughter follows me all the way down the hall.

Fable

It's so cold outside and gloomy, the sky full of dark, foreboding clouds and that ever-present wind. I pull my coat tight around me, following Drew as we walk through the cemetery. He's taking a winding path through the gravestones and I try my hardest not to look at them, but I can't resist. Some of them are beautiful, with actual pictures on them, heartbreaking messages, and even statues.

And flowers. Flowers everywhere, real and fake, bright and cheery, dark and somber. Some are holiday-themed. I see remnants of Halloween ribbon, plenty of autumnal colors. Rusty reds and oranges and harvest yellows.

I feel better, seeing all the color, the benches that people put out there to actually spend time with the loved ones they've lost. Death is a terrible thing but it's also such a part of life. I don't like thinking about it, our mortal selves.

It's easier to pretend we'll live forever.

"Here it is."

Drew's deep, somber voice makes me glance up and I see he's stopped directly in front of a small gravestone that lies close to the ground.

Slowly I approach, stopping just at his side, and I let my gaze settle on the words written across the stone:

Vanessa Adele Callahan

Born September 30th, 2007

Died November 27th, 2010

Forever in our hearts . . .

There's a little picture of Vanessa in the upper right-hand corner. Her hair is dark like Drew's; she has a big smile on her face and her blue eyes twinkle.

She was adorable.

I glance over at Drew and see him staring at her picture, his hands in his jacket's pockets, his expression bleak. Full of sadness. I want to comfort him, want to draw him into my arms and whisper that everything's going to be all right, but I don't feel like it's my place.

Plus, he needs to do this. He told me so on the drive

over. He wanted a few moments where he did nothing else but look at her grave and think of her. Talk to her in his mind.

I agreed, because who am I to judge his grieving practices? We all mourn differently. Personally, I wouldn't want to come out here, especially since his sister died at such a young age.

Curiosity creeps over me again and I try to ignore it. I really want to know how she died. I don't know why it's bothering me so much, but everyone in this family is so damn secretive about everything. This one little detail is major and I want to know.

I *have* to know.

A shuddering breath leaves Drew, and I can't take it anymore. Stepping closer to him, I grab hold of his arm and squeeze it, wanting him to know I'm there for him if he needs anything. He hauls me in closer, his arm going around my shoulders, and the next thing I know, he's embracing me, his face buried in my hair, his arms wound so tight around me I can hardly breathe.

But I let him hang on to me. He needs the comfort. I do, too.

"It's my fault," I hear him murmur against my hair. "I was watching her outside while my dad took a phone call. And then . . . then I left."

A prickly sensation skitters down my spine and I try to

keep myself relaxed so he doesn't catch on that what he's said disturbs me. Yet I want him to be open with me, not close himself off.

"It was an accident." I have no idea whether this is true since no one's told me, but it seems the right thing to say. "It wasn't anyone's fault."

"No." He sets me away from him, his blue eyes blazing as he stares down at me. His body vibrates with emotion and he runs a shaky hand through his hair. "Did Adele tell you what happened? Did she?"

"I—no." I shake my head, gasping when he grasps me by the shoulders and gives me a little shake. "She didn't tell me anything. Only that she died."

He pushes me away, cursing under his breath, and I stumble, stunned that he would treat me that way. He's walking away, his head down, his strides quick, and I follow him, confused and angry and suddenly wishing I'd never come with him to this horrible, depressing place.

"Where are you going?" I yell, huffing and puffing against the wind and the cold, pissed that his long legs give him such an advantage.

"I need to be alone."

"Give me a break," I mutter, increasing my speed. "You can't avoid the bad shit forever, you know," I tell him.

He whirls on me, his face contorted with so much conflicting emotion, it's as if he's a different person. "You don't know me. I *don't* avoid the bad shit. I fucking live it every single day of my life!"

I'm taken aback by his outburst, again with the show of emotion. Even though he's taking all of his anger and turmoil out on me, this has to be good for him, right? "You don't have to deal with it by yourself, you know. It's okay to grieve and talk about her."

"I grieve and it's full of guilt. It's *my* fault my baby sister got inside the pool area and drowned. I was supposed to stay outside and watch her, but I—I didn't. I thought the gate was closed." He thrusts both hands through his hair, clutching at the dark strands as he stares unseeingly at me. "It's my fault *and* her fault."

"Her fault? Do you mean Vanessa?" She was practically a baby! How could he say that?

"No, fuck, of course not. *Her* fault. God." His voice catches on a sob and I realize tears are streaming down his cheeks. Seeing them, seeing him so distressed, makes my heart ache, but I'm afraid to go to him. Afraid he'll only push me away and I can't stand the thought of that. Yet it hurts to watch him grieving alone, thinking this is somehow all his fault and whoever else's.

I'm so confused. And honestly?

I'm afraid to ask.

"Tell me what happened," I demand, deciding to be brave and face this head-on. "How did your sister die?"

Drew wipes furiously at his face, banishing the tears as we head back toward Vanessa's gravesite. I give him a moment, sitting on a bench nearby. The tree branches above my head wave with the wind, and I shiver beneath my too-thin coat, watching him as he begins to pace directly in front of me.

"I was outside. Hanging out with my dad and enjoying the sun. That Thanksgiving break it was warmer than usual, and I was riding high after doing so well during my first year on the team." His voice trails off and he looks lost in thought. "Adele had been gone most of the day, shopping for Christmas presents. She asked my dad to watch Vanessa and we were playing with her. She'd run back and forth across the back patio, giggling nonstop. It took her awhile to warm up to me, you know? Because I wasn't home much, but I always got her to come around."

I say nothing, letting him take his time to tell this story. He needs to get it out, no matter how painful it must be for him to relive the day. I'd rather comfort him and tell him we'll talk about it another time, but when?

"My dad got a phone call. He'd been working on a big merger that had taken him months to put together and he had to take the call. He told me I needed to watch Vanessa, never let her out of my sight, and of course I said I would." He releases a shuddering sigh and closes his eyes. "She played hide-and-go-seek with me and we were laughing, I was teasing her. I knew my dad wasn't too far off—I could hear him talking on the phone.

"Adele was suddenly at the door and she asked me . . . she asked me to come inside with her. I told her I couldn't, that I had to watch Vanessa, but she convinced me Vanessa would be fine. My dad was right there. And he was, I swear he was. So I went in and . . . and Vanessa somehow got inside the gated area that surrounds the pool and she fell in. Turns out my dad had walked to the front of the house, but I didn't know it then. He didn't realize I'd left Vanessa alone. I thought he had her and he thought I had her . . ."

Drew falls apart. Literally crumples to the ground on his knees in front of his sister's grave, his shoulders heaving as he hunches over the gravestone as if in prayer. "I'm sorry. I fucked up and I'm so goddamned sorry."

I go to him. Get down on my knees and wrap my arms around him as best I can. He turns to me, slinging his arms around my neck and pressing his face against my chest. I can feel the dampness of his tears against my skin and I stroke his head, my fingers tangling in his hair as I try my best to soothe him.

We sit like that for several long, silent minutes, his body trembling with emotion as he quietly cries against me. I let him, feel the tears and the sadness well up inside of me, too, and I cry with him. Silent tears that purge me, connecting me to Drew as I feel his raw, all-encompassing grief and pain.

This isn't all that plagues him, I know. I can sense there's more, much more, and he's holding back for fear I might freak out. Or worse, think less of him.

It has to do with Adele. And I think I know what it is.

I'm just not ready to face it yet.

CHAPTER 13

Day 6 (Black Friday), 11:00 p.m.

> *It's the people who know you the best who can hurt you*
> *the most.*
> —Drew Callahan

Drew

I'm desperate to lose myself in her so I can forget.

After the cemetery, we grabbed some fast food for lunch, then headed back home. There wasn't much talking between us, and I couldn't have held a conversation if I tried. I'm exhausted, both emotionally and physically, and she knows it. Fable doesn't push, doesn't ask for any explanations unless she deems it necessary.

Like her asking what happened the day Vanessa drowned. Hard to believe, but it felt good getting everything off of my chest. I've never talked about my sister's death with anyone. Not my parents, no one. I've held that inside me for two years and once I started talking, it was like a dam broke.

I cried. I mourned. I told my story and was so damn thankful when she didn't flinch, didn't condemn, didn't judge. She just held me and let me cry, like I was some sort of big baby.

Damn it. I refuse to judge myself, get down on myself for having fucking emotions. I lost my baby sister on my watch. I have every right to cry and rage if I want.

We slept the rest of the afternoon away. Together. Curled up in the middle of my bed, our arms slung around each other, a blanket drawn up over us. All afternoon through most of the evening we remained like this, and I knew we both needed it. Neither of us has slept much this week while in Carmel.

We leave tomorrow, the day my family is acknowledging as the two-year anniversary of my sister's death. I'm glad to get out of here, but unsure what life's going to bring Fable and me when we get back home.

I'm afraid of what I might do. What she might do. What we both might do together to screw everything up.

My cell pings and I know without looking who it is. My dad or Adele, the very last two people I want to talk to. I scoot over and sit up, reaching for my phone. The lamp on the dresser across the room is still on, casting its dim glow.

Glancing at my cell, I see that yep, it's my dad who sent the text, and just as I'm about to read it, the phone starts to ring. Again, it's my dad.

"Sorry I haven't returned your calls," I immediately say, feeling bad. He's having a tough time of it, too, and I shouldn't shut him out, no matter how easy he makes it.

"Don't you dare hang up on me." *Fuck*, it's Adele.

"What do you want?" I keep my voice low, trying my best not to disturb Fable, but she rustles under the blanket, turning away so her back is to me.

I have no idea if she's awake or not, but I have no plans to say anything to Adele that Fable might question later. It's bad enough I confessed what happened with Vanessa today. No way can I dump any more on her.

"You're coming with us tomorrow, right? To Vanessa's grave?"

"I went already today."

Dead silence answers me and I say nothing in return. I'm not going to be the one who says something first. I'm tired of being at this woman's bidding. It's gone on far too long.

"Did you go with her?"

"I did."

A hiss escapes her. "How dare you bring her to my little girl's grave."

"She's my sister, damn it. I can bring my *girlfriend* to her grave."

"She's not your . . . *God*." Adele seems to choke on her words. "You're coming with us tomorrow. I need you there."

"We leave tomorrow. I can't. That's why I went today." Not exactly true, but the explanation works.

"You'll disappoint your father." She lowers her voice, until it sounds like she's almost crooning to me. "You don't want to disappoint him, do you? You're always such a good boy, Andrew. You always do what I say. What I ask from you."

My skin is literally crawling at how she's talking to me and I close my eyes, take a deep breath, and pray I don't fall apart. Yet again. I've been on a nonstop emotional bender since I came back here. I knew it would be bad. I didn't expect all this, though. "I'm not going with you, Adele. It's time to cut the ties for good." I hang up on her before she can say anything else.

I look at Fable to find that she's rolled back over so she's facing me again, those intense green eyes watching my every move. My stomach bottoms out and I wonder how much she heard.

"She giving you a hard time?" she asks softly.

I nod. Don't say a word.

Pushing the blanket off her body, she gets up on her knees and comes to me, resting her hands on my shoulders, her face in mine. Her lids lower and she stares at my mouth. I can see the rapid rise and fall of her chest, feel the comforting warmth of her touch. This girl, she just . . .

Does it for me.

But I don't know how to put it in words and tell her.

"Thank you for everything today," she says, surprising me.

I frown as I reach out and tuck a strand of silky hair behind her ear. "I should be thanking *you* for all that you did for me."

"Yes, you should." A tremulous smile curves her lips. "But I wanted to thank you for being so honest. For telling me about your sister and sharing that part of your life with me. I know it wasn't easy."

My fingers linger on her soft cheek and I stroke my thumb back and forth. "Thank you for being there for me. Listening to me." *And holding me in your arms and letting me cry.*

She crawls on top of me, her legs on either side of my thighs, and I automatically grab her, splaying my hands across her perfect ass and hauling her in close. God, she feels amazing like this, nestled up so close against me you couldn't fit a slice of paper between us. "Drew." Her voice is whisper soft as she leans in and presses a gentle kiss to my lips. "This is our last night here. Together."

My body hurts at the realization. This is it. We go back to our regular lives tomorrow evening. I can't wait for this torture to end, yet knowing that I won't have Fable pretending to be my fake girlfriend any longer . . .

That stings. More than I care to admit.

Sliding one hand up her back, I slip it beneath her sweater so I'm caressing bare, smooth skin. She trembles beneath my touch as she leans in, her hair falling all around our faces, her lips hovering just above mine. I know what she wants.

I want the same thing.

Tilting my head back against the headboard, I cup her nape and pull her in, our mouths meeting in a soft, lingering kiss. I sneak my tongue out and lick her upper lip, then trace the edge of her lower lip, savoring her sweet, decadent taste. A little moan escapes her and I take the kiss deeper, clutching the back of her head harder as I plunder her mouth with my tongue.

I'm overcome with my need for her. I've never felt this way before, and memories of our night together flood me. When she so selflessly brought me to orgasm and never asked for anything in return. I want to do the same for her. Give her whatever she wants, whatever she needs from me.

I want to be with her, our naked bodies entwined all night long.

I also need to make sure she wants this. Wants me . . .

"Are you hungry? I mean, we only just woke up." I say this after I break apart from her kiss, my lips tingling and already eager to be back on hers. I think I'm trying to give her an out, I don't know. Which is so stupid, but I don't want us to get in too deep only for her to back off.

I know I'm ready. But is she? Really?

Pulling away from me, she reaches for the hem of her sweater and tugs it up and over her head, tossing it onto the floor. She has on a simple white bra, trimmed with lace and the tiniest white satin bow in the center. So innocent and sweet looking, though my thoughts are far from that as I stare at her, contemplating how I can get her out of that damn bra without looking like I'm moving too fast.

"I'm hungry for you," she whispers, her eyes glowing, her swollen mouth glistening from our kiss. "Take off your shirt, Drew."

Without hesitation I reach for the bottom of my shirt and tear it off, leaving it beside me on the bed. Her gaze never leaves mine as she wraps herself around me, her legging-covered legs curving around my waist, her arms going around my neck. She buries her hands in my hair and I close my eyes, absorbing her scent, the feel of her warm body so close to mine. Our upper bodies are skin on skin, her bra the only barrier, and the satiny-smooth fabric arouses me further as she brushes her chest against mine.

As our mouths find each other, I'm overwhelmed with emotion for this girl. I've craved this connection with her for days. Hell, I've craved this sort of connection with someone for years, always too afraid to believe in it.

But I'm a believer now. Thanks to my one-week girlfriend.

Thanks to Fable.

Fable

Drew Callahan truly has the most beautiful male body I've ever laid eyes on, and I'm embarrassed to admit I've laid eyes on more than my fair share of masculine bodies.

I was so distracted by his ever-persistent mouth locked with mine that it took a while to break away from his kiss, and now I'm even happier to soak up all of this exposed muscle and sinew. Last time we were together, we were shrouded in darkness. Too scared to look at each other for fear of what we really might see.

Now I want to see all. Everything. I want to stare into his eyes the first time he enters me. I want to keep our gazes locked when he makes me come. I want to hear him whisper my name when I make *him* come . . .

A shiver moves through me as I slide my fingers across

his broad shoulders, down his arms, lingering on his rock-hard biceps, skimming over the dark hair that covers his forearms. He remains utterly still, but I can feel his hot eyes on me, devouring me as I intently search his flesh with my hands. I touch his chest, the tips of my index fingers gliding over his nipples simultaneously, and he jumps a little, making me smile.

But my smile fades as I become enraptured with every bump and groove of his washboard stomach. I slow my search, let my hands completely map his abs, and I feel his muscles quiver beneath my touch.

Lifting my head, I find him watching me, his brows raised, his mouth quirked in a half-smile. This is by far the happiest I've seen him since the afternoon he took me to lunch and kissed me in a fairy-tale alley while it rained, with white lights twinkling all around us.

Without a word I press my lips to his, keeping my eyes open until his shutter closed, and I find myself falling so easily under his spell. This kiss is hungrier, more urgent, and I let him take the lead, revel in how he rests his big hand at the top of my chest before sliding it up to lightly touch my throat in a wholly possessive gesture that has me reeling.

That same hand slides back down, his fingers dipping beneath the loose strap of my bra, pushing it off my shoulder. He does the same to the other strap, magically removing the bra from me within seconds, and my bare breasts are crushed to his chest, my nipples hard against the warmth of his skin.

"I want you," he whispers in my ear, sending shivers careening down my spine. "So bad it's killing me, Fable."

I love that he says my name in the same breath that he declares he wants me. Rather than become lost in the darkness or blinded by the past, he's here. With me now, touching me and kissing me, slowly grinding his erection against me. I'm completely absorbed by him, lost within him, and there's no place I'd rather be.

He grabs hold of my waist and pushes me down onto the bed so I'm flat on my back, his hands pressed on either side of my head on the mattress as he leans over, his mouth never leaving mine. In this position, he's not as close as I want him, and I curl my legs around his hips, desperate to draw him near.

Breaking our kiss, he pulls away and slides down the length of my body, his hands at the waistband of my thin black leggings as he slowly, patiently tugs them down, taking my panties along with them. I'm trembling, my breaths are coming too fast, and I stare up at the ceiling, biting the inside of my lip when his fingers brush against my thighs, my knees, my calves as he strips me. I feel his breath against the very center of me and I close my eyes, dizziness swamping me when I feel those large hands of his pushing my thighs apart.

He's studying me down there and I don't know what to think, what to say. He releases a ragged breath, his hands gripping my hips, and then he's kissing my chest, running his lips all over my flesh until I feel his tongue lick first one nipple, then another.

I can't take it any longer. I'm not one to remain silent in bed—I never have been, not that I'm a total screamer. But his touch, his mouth on my skin feels so good, I arch into him and cry out. I'm on complete sensation overload, totally naked and exposed, and I've never felt so cherished. So alive.

"You're beautiful," he whispers against my breasts as he worships them with his mouth. I sink my hand into his hair and hold him to me, writhing beneath his busy lips and tongue. I'm still baffled. Honestly, I don't quite know how we got to this point. I hated him on sight. I did this only for the money. I thought he was a fucked-up mess. I *still* think he's a fucked-up mess.

But so am I. And he's so beautiful, so thoughtful, so vulnerable. We can be a mess together. I want to heal him. I know I can heal him.

This joining of our bodies is the first step.

"Hold on," he murmurs. I open my eyes and his face is

in mine. He steals a quick kiss and removes himself from me, getting off the bed. "I'll be right back."

I watch him leave and I throw my arm over my eyes, trying my best to calm my racing heart, my accelerated breath. My body is so ramped up, it won't take much to send me right over the edge. I'm trembling, so full of adrenaline and desire and whatever other mysterious emotions are swirling inside my body. I've never, ever felt like this before. Ever.

The realization leaves me breathless.

Drew slips back inside the room minutes later, shutting the door and turning the lock into place. I watch him quietly as he walks toward the bed and sets a small box of condoms on the bedside table. I meet his gaze, one eyebrow raised, and he smiles.

"We lucked out. There's a box in the bathroom under the sink. They're always there, like towels and shampoo and soap. They keep this guesthouse busy, like a hotel sometimes, I swear. My dad always has business clients staying here."

Huh. Well, if the Callahans always have guests staying with them, at least they're providing a safe haven.

I can't ponder the condom issue too long, though. Not when Drew is busy undoing the snap and zipper on his jeans, letting them fall from his hips to a heap around his ankles before he kicks them off. My mouth goes dry at the sight of him, how he fills out his black cotton boxer briefs so perfectly.

And then he's taking those off, too, and I'm staring unabashedly, marveling at how big he really is and how that might feel when he finally joins his body with mine.

As in, it might hurt. All of a sudden, I'm scared shitless.

I swear he can sense my change in mood and he tries to reassure me. He gathers me in his strong arms, holding me close. I shut my eyes and bury my head against his firm chest, breathe in his clean, unique scent. He's gentle, he's tender, but he's also persistent and soon we're kissing, searching each other's bodies with busy hands, rolling around the mattress like a couple of kids in a playful wrestling match.

But there's nothing playful about this big, muscular man pinning me to the bed, my arms spread above my head, his fingers locked around my wrists as he studies me with those beautiful blue eyes.

He slipped the condom on only moments ago. I know he's ready. I'm ready. But I'm still nervous. This is such a turning point in our relationship, something we can never go back on. I won't forget him or this night. He's permanently writing himself in my personal history.

"There's no going back," he whispers, as if he can read my mind.

I slowly nod, too overcome to find words.

"Once I'm inside you, you're mine."

Oh. I never, ever thought hearing a guy say that would arouse me so much, but it does. I've always thought of myself as an independent person. I belong to no one.

But the idea of belonging to Drew fills me with so much joy, I'm afraid I might burst.

"I want you to be mine, Fable." Loosening his hold on my wrists, he dips his head, nuzzling my cheek, my nose. It's the sweetest, sexiest gesture, and I moan as I circle my arms around his neck and cradle him close.

"I want to be yours," I answer in a breathy whisper. "I want to belong to you, Drew. Only you."

He kisses me, at the same time sliding his body into mine. Inch by thick inch, taking my breath away with the sheer size of him, and I tense up, holding my breath as he rocks deeper and deeper into me.

"I'm hurting you." He presses sweet, quick kisses all over my face. "Relax. Breathe."

I do as he urges, trying my best to ease the tension from my abdomen, and it becomes easier, Drew pushing inside me. His entire body is tense from holding back, his skin covered in a fine mist of sweat, and I wiggle my hips, spread my legs a little bit wider, allowing him to sink deeper.

We both groan at the sensation and start to move. Together. Tentatively at first, learning each other's rhythm, tuning our bodies until they become synced in a fluid, easy motion. He rocks into me, harder. Harder still, making me lose my mind with his every thrust. I'm losing myself—my brain is fuzzy, my thoughts distant. All I can do is feel. The incredible wave threatens, I know I'm about to go completely under, but then he surprises me.

Drew drags me into a sitting position, his back against the bed's headboard, my legs wound around his waist, much like we sat only moments before, when we were still fully clothed. Only now, we're naked, both physically and emotionally, our bodies connected, his flesh buried so deep in mine, I feel as if he's embedded in me.

"I was losing you." He knows me so well. "And I didn't want you to forget who you're with. Who's about to make you come." His voice is deep, so deep, as is his cock, and I shudder all around him. Excited by his possessive tone, thrilled by his sweet words.

Drew completely undoes me—with a look, with a word, with a thrust of his body, with a lick of his tongue. Every single thing he does to me devastates. Intoxicates. Renews.

Every single thing inside of me.

"I'll never forget who I'm with," I whisper against his lips before I kiss him. His hands are gripping my hips, pulling me down, and I work with him, eager for the explosion, yet wanting to draw it out just a little bit longer.

He curves his hand around the back of my head, his

fingers knotted in my hair in such a tight grip it stings. But I relish the pain, how it makes me feel alive. How being in Drew's arms, having him buried deep inside me, makes me feel.

Alive. Cherished. Loved.

He breathes my name against my lips and I know he's close. So am I. I angle myself just so, rubbing against him, rocking into him, and I fall apart with a little cry, my entire body shaking. He tumbles right after me, his body quivering as he groans in exquisite agony, his arm clutching me so tight around my waist, I almost can't breathe.

We cling to each other for long minutes after, our bodies still shuddering, our breathing slowly evening out. I don't want to let him go, don't want to let him out of my body, and I know I'm being ridiculous.

But I can't help myself. Drew Callahan has forever changed me, and the knowledge both invigorates and terrifies me. There is still so much I don't know.

Still so much I need him to reveal to me. Scary parts of his life I'm frightened to learn. But the truth . . . don't they say the truth will set you free?

I want to free Drew from the prison his past has put him in. And the only way I can do that is if I know what happened.

And tomorrow, I am determined to find out.

I have to.

CHAPTER 14

Day 7 (Departure), 9:00 a.m.

> *The course of true love never did run smooth.*
> —William Shakespeare

Drew

We slept in, our naked bodies entwined, her back to my front and my hands cupping her breasts. With her fragrant hair in my face and her legs tangled with mine, I woke up hard as steel and ready to take her again.

Which I did.

I've had sex with Fable four times since last night. Every single time is better than the last and I am so gone over this girl, it's pathetic. Amazing.

She finally urges me out of bed, telling me we need to get a move on, and she's right. Four-hour drive on a busy travel day, I know it's probably going to take longer than usual.

Plus, I want to escape so I don't have to face Adele. Or my father. How awful is that? I love my dad, but today . . . today will be hard for him. And I don't know if I can deal with it. I actually feel guilty, being so happy on this day— though it's not the exact day of Vanessa's death, it's close enough—yet I want to fight it off.

I'm tired of the guilt and the exhaustion. The worry and the shame. For once in my life, I just had sex with a beautiful woman all night long and I want to revel in it. I want to be with her, touch her, tell her how much she means to me, instead of running away and hiding from it all.

Fable is so fucking good for me, I can't ever let her go.

We shower together because I'm greedy and so is she. I slip my fingers between her legs and gently bring her to orgasm, my mouth fused with hers the whole time, swallowing her gasps and moans as the warm water beats down on us. And then she drops to her knees and takes me into her mouth, her lips wrapped around the head of my cock, her tongue mapping every bit of me until I come with a shuddering gust of breath.

That in itself is a major turning point. My past experiences have made me hate blow jobs. Only because they filled me with such revulsion when the memories came. The shame, the horror at how easily I gave in to one woman's insistence that what we were doing wasn't wrong. That there was nothing to be ashamed of.

She *was* wrong. I knew what we did wasn't right, yet I couldn't control myself, my urges, my responses to her. She knew how to arouse me and I hated that.

I hated what she turned me into. Her sexual toy, a plaything to take out and fuck and jerk off and use until I was spent and sick to my stomach. More than once after she left me, I contemplated suicide. But I couldn't do it. I was too scared, too afraid of what might happen if I lived after all.

So I turned into a shell. A robot going through the motions, living my life, doing what I was supposed to and getting ahead just fine. Keeping everyone at a distance, embracing football and nothing else.

Until this girl came along and intrigued me. Surprised me. Intoxicated me.

Stripped me completely.

"You're insatiable," she tells me after we towel each other off.

Her words render me frozen. Adele said much the same thing that night at the country club. Those words had enraged me. Shamed me.

Much as they do now.

The smile falls from Fable's perfect lips as I stare at her, trying to get my anger under control. I can't lose it, not like this. Not after spending the most perfect night of my life with her. "What's wrong?" she asks.

I shake my head and exit the bathroom, heading for my room so I can change. I'm already packed and pretty much ready to go, save for a few things. I need to get out of here, away from this house. Away from this life. It's not a part of me anymore, and I can feel its thorny tendrils winding around my mind, trying to stick in me and never let me escape.

Minutes later Fable is in my room, hastily dressed, her jeans still unsnapped, her shirt thrown on haphazardly. She straightens it out around her slim shoulders, offering tantalizing glimpses of her skin, and I'm momentarily distracted.

But I realize her probing gaze is locked on me and she's not going to let me escape. "Tell me what's wrong."

"I'm just . . . ready to go." That's a good enough answer. It has to be.

"Something happened back there. I want to know what." She crosses her arms in front of her chest, something I haven't seen her do in days, and I realize it's a defensive gesture. She's trying to be tough, showing me that she won't back down.

Well, I'm not backing down either. We can't have this conversation here. Now. "Let it go, Fable. Seriously."

"No." She steps forward and shoves me right in the chest with both hands. "I'm tired of pretending there's nothing wrong. I'm sick of you blowing up and freaking out and then telling me you're fine. I know you're still grieving for your sister. I know you feel guilty over her death, and I get that. But there's more going on here. Something else happened that you're not telling me. And I really need you to tell me, Drew."

I slowly shake my head, the air leaving my lungs all at once. "I—I can't."

"You *have* to." She reaches out to shove me again and I grab her wrists, stopping her. "I need to know. How else can I help you get past this?"

"Trust me, you don't want to know." I let go of her and turn to my bag that's sitting on the bed but she grabs my arm, jerking me around so I'm facing her once more.

"Don't shut me out. I'm here for *you*. After everything we've been through, after what we've just shared." She sighs and closes her eyes for the briefest moment, as if she's completely overcome. "I've bared my body and my soul to you, and I have never, ever done that for anyone before. So please, I'm *begging* you. Tell me what the hell happened!"

I stare at her, desperate to confess. Scared of her reaction. I part my lips, but the words won't come. It's like the world is sitting on my chest, crushing my heart and turning it to dust.

"Can I guess?" Her voice is so soft, I lean in to hear her. "I . . . I have my suspicions. Can I ask you questions and you answer me yes or no?"

What she suggests is the coward's way out. And considering I'm pretty much a coward at this very moment, it's the only way out for me.

So I nod.

Breathing deep, she takes a step back, leaning against the dresser behind her. "Whatever happened to you in your past happened here, didn't it? Not in the guesthouse but here, at this house. Not at school, not anywhere else, right?"

I swallow hard and nod once.

"Okay." She presses her lips together, her eyes clouded with what looks like worry. "I think . . . it has to do with Adele, doesn't it?"

I'm silent. Paralyzed. I want to say yes. I want to run. She's so close. So close to figuring it out and then I realize she probably already *has* figured it out, and I'm so full of shame, I want to throw up.

"Yeah," I say on a ragged breath, rubbing the back of my hand across my mouth. I swear I'm going to puke.

Fear is in her eyes as she looks at me. Sympathy and

worry and tears I don't want her to shed for me. "She—she molested you, didn't she?"

I shake my head, shocked at her choice of words. "She didn't molest me. I knew exactly what I was doing with her."

Fable's mouth drops open. "What?"

"We were having an affair. That's it. No molestation, no her touching me when I was a little kid. She went after me, seduced me, I fell for her, and we had an affair for years." I spit the last words out, so disgusted with myself I can hardly see straight. "There, Fable. There's your answer. Now that you have it, what do you think? I'm disgusting, right? Sneaking around with my stepmom, having her slip inside my room in the middle of the night. Fucking her furiously again and again. She always knew how to get me hard and I couldn't stand how easily she had control over me." I'm shaking, my breath is stuttering in my lungs, and my teeth are chattering. I can't fucking believe I just said all that. I told her everything. *Everything*.

Fable just stands there gaping at me, her eyes still flooded with tears. "How—how old were you when this first started?"

"Almost fifteen." Horny as fuck, too. Adele knew it. She was beautiful, mysterious. She flattered me, flirted with me, and I responded. She's only eleven years older than me; she'd tell me we had more in common than she and my dad did, and then the next thing I knew, she was sneaking into my room in the middle of the night, touching me. Going down on me, making me come so hard I thought I would black out.

I was young, full of hormones, and eager to fuck. Constantly. And despite the shame and the hatred I had for myself and for her, I secretly wanted her to get me off. Sought out her attention because for a brief moment, I felt wanted, desired, loved.

And after, when she'd leave me alone in my room, I was ashamed. Disgusted. Full of hate for her and for myself. For my dad, who was completely blind to it all. For my mom, who died when I was young and wasn't there to protect me.

"You were a child and she took advantage of you, Drew. That's not an affair between two consenting adults, that's your stepmom *molesting* you." Her voice is shaking, her entire body shakes, much like mine, and then she does the craziest thing.

She runs to me and grabs hold of me so tight, like she's never going to let me go. She's crying, sobbing into my shirt, and I slowly slip my arms around her and hold her close. I have no tears, there's no sadness welling up inside me. I'm emotionless. Blank. I think I might be in shock.

I just confessed my darkest, dirtiest secret and Fable didn't run. She didn't laugh, she didn't mock me, she didn't point any accusatory fingers.

For once in my life, I feel like I've finally found someone who understands.

Fable

I knew it. As much as I didn't want to face it, I knew the problem stemmed from Adele. As the week wore on, more and more clues were revealed, and my suspicions grew.

And now they've been confirmed.

Hatred fills me, so overwhelmingly strong I'm dizzy with it. I hate that woman for what she's done to Drew. How she continues to torture him. She's disgusting. She's a fucking child molester who should be in jail, for the love of God, for the way she took advantage of her stepson.

I hate her with everything inside of me.

"We need to go," I say against his chest, my voice muffled. I pull away so I can look up at him, and I notice that his face is completely devoid of emotion. He's in shutdown mode, and I can't chastise him since he's most likely using it as a coping mechanism.

The minute we get back home, I'm telling him he needs to go to a professional therapist. Get what happened to him out of his mind once and for all. Not that he can ever let his past experiences go for good, but he can at least talk to someone. Seek help so he can better cope with everything.

"Drew." I shake his arms and his eyes focus on me once more. "We need to leave. Now."

"You're right. Let's go."

I run to my room and toss everything in my bag, then zip it up. I grab my purse, then the sweatshirt I'm going to wear, and glance around the room, making sure I haven't left anything.

It really wouldn't matter if I did. I so want out of here, I don't even care.

I wait for Drew in the living room, keeping watch out the window, my gaze zeroed in on the main house. They haven't left yet for whatever they planned to do to mourn Vanessa's death. I see the Range Rover parked out in the drive, as if Drew's dad pulled it out earlier in preparation. At least it's not blocking Drew's truck.

Thank God.

"Do you want to say goodbye to your dad?" I ask when he comes into the living area, his bag slung over his shoulder, his expression still somewhat blank.

He slowly shakes his head. "I'll text him. Have they left yet?"

"No." The panic is blatant in my voice and I clear my throat, irritated with myself. "Drew, I don't think it's a good idea if we go over there . . ."

"I don't either," he interrupts.

Relief sweeps through me and we head out to his truck with hurried steps, my movements downright frantic as I toss my bag into the narrow backseat of his extended cab. He climbs into the truck the same time I do and we slam our doors in unison, Drew jabbing the key into the ignition.

We're so close to being out of here, I can almost taste it. I've never been so happy to leave a place as I am at this very moment.

"Andrew!"

I jerk my head to the left and watch in disbelief as Adele runs toward the truck, stopping at the driver's-side door. She's smacking the glass with her fist, yelling for him to roll down the window, and he stares at her, his hand on the gear shift, ready to put the truck in reverse.

"Don't do it," I murmur. "Don't open the window. She doesn't deserve your attention anymore, Drew."

"What if she tells my dad?" His voice is so small, he sounds like a little boy and my heart breaks for him. His pain has become mine.

"Who cares? You're not wrong in this situation. She is."

Keeping his head bent, he reaches out and hits the button so the window slowly rolls down. "What do you want?" he asks her coldly.

"Just . . . please come with us. I want you there, Andrew." She flicks her cold, hard gaze at me briefly and I stare back. Just as cold, just as hard.

I want to tear her apart, I hate her so much.

"I already visited her grave yesterday. I paid my sister my respect. What more do you want from me?" His voice is like ice, his glare just as frosty as he turns it on her, and it's as though she's completely oblivious.

"There's so much more you don't know, and I—I need to tell you. Privately. It's important, Andrew. Please."

"Stop calling him that." I can't help it—I have to make her stop. I can't stand the way she says his full name.

"It's his name." Her voice is flat. "And who the hell are you to tell me what to do?"

"Don't talk to her like that." His low voice is a warning, but it still doesn't seem to affect Adele.

"She's nothing, Andrew. Worthless. Why do you spend time with her? Is she good in bed? Does she spread her legs for you constantly and that's why you keep her around?" Adele sounds downright manic. I refuse to let her insults affect me whatsoever.

She's so beneath me for what she's done to Drew, she deserves to rot in hell.

"At least I'm not some child-molesting piece of shit," I mutter under my breath.

The gasp I hear from Adele clearly indicates that I didn't mutter low enough. "What did you say, you little bitch?"

Holy shit, I've stepped in it now.

"She knows, Adele," Drew interjects harshly. "She knows everything."

The heavy silence that settles over the three of us is almost painful. I can't look at her. I keep my focus on my trembling knees, trying my best to keep my breathing even and controlled. I glance at Drew out of the corner of my eye and see the tic in his jaw; the way he's gripping the steering wheel so tight, his knuckles are white.

"Well." Her voice squeaks and she gives a little cough. "So. You told her everything, hmm? She knows about our little affair?"

"Molesting a fifteen-year-old boy is a far cry from having an affair." I clamp my lips shut and close my eyes. My mom always said my big mouth would get me in trouble.

I guess she's right.

"Fine—you want her to know everything, then I'll go ahead and tell you what I wanted to say in private in front of your big-mouthed whore instead." Her voice is sweetness and light, so unnerving I can't help but lift my head and look at her.

I don't like what I see. There's a murderous glow in her

eyes, and her mouth is curved upward in a crazed smile. She's clearly on the verge of losing it.

"We should go," I whisper to Drew, and without a word he starts the engine.

"Don't you want to hear what I have to tell you?" she asks in her creepy singsong voice.

"Not really." He keeps his gaze trained on the steering wheel.

"That's too bad. Because it's about Vanessa."

He turns to look at her, as do I. "What about her?"

"I've been trying to tell you this for what feels like forever; the timing was just never right. But you need to know. I've always felt it was the truth . . . I wasn't sure. I know it now, though. Without a doubt, I know."

"Spit it out, Adele."

My stomach is churning as I wait. Fear makes my palms clammy and I clutch at my knees, scared out of my mind at what she's about to say.

"Vanessa wasn't your sister, Andrew." Adele pauses, the smile she shoots my direction devastating. "She was your daughter."

CHAPTER 15

Day 7 (Departure), 1:30 p.m.

> *Where there is love, there is pain.*
> —Spanish proverb

Fable

More than four hours later, and I still don't know what to say.

I'm in a perpetual state of shock over Adele's devastating confession. I'm not the one who's most traumatically affected by it, either. I'm scared to death by the way Drew is taking it. Which is zero reaction whatsoever.

He's cold as ice. Expressionless. Emotionless. Void of anything and everything.

I've spent six full days and nights with him. I've seen him at his lowest and highest points, his most angry and his most caring, yet I've never seen him act like this.

I don't know what to do for him. And he won't talk to me.

It ends up being the longest, quietest four-plus hours of my life. Traffic was brutal, the weather shitty, with slick roads and heavy rain, making it nearly impossible for him to see through the windshield.

He flicked on the radio at the very start of our journey, a clear indicator that he didn't want to talk, so I didn't press. But I wanted to. Oh, how I wanted to! There were so many questions and I had no answers.

Was Adele telling the truth? Had Vanessa really been Drew's daughter? Did his father—her husband—have any sort of clue? Had he been aware of their affair? Exactly how long had it gone on, anyway?

From my calculations, she'd done this to him for a long time. At least four years. In the bits that he told me about the day Vanessa died, I have a feeling Adele dragged him into the house and had her way with him. So while they were fucking, Vanessa drowned.

Brutal, but the truth—I can feel it. Hence that extra heaping dose of guilt he piles on himself.

I'm not angry at him, though, and I can't hate him for what happened. It's not his fault, no matter how much he thinks it is. She trapped him into this crazy, sick relationship, and he didn't know how to get out of it. He was a child when she started playing her twisted game.

It's a wonder he was able to be with me at all last night.

I slept fitfully the last hour or so of the drive, and I wake up with a jolt when the truck comes to a complete stop and he shuts off the engine. I lift my head and peer out the window, discovering we're in the parking lot of my apartment complex.

Yay. I'm home.

"We're here," he says, his deep voice deathly quiet. "Need help with your bag?"

I stare at him in disbelief. "Is this really how we're going to end it?"

His gaze meets mine and it's full of so much pain, I almost look away. But I refuse. He's not going to win. I refuse to let him drive me away. "You heard what she said, Fable. No way do I expect you to stick around after that."

"You really think that little of me? Really?" God, he infuriates me! I want to smack him and hug him, all at once. "Fine."

I reach behind me and grab my duffel bag, then throw open the door, climbing out of the truck so quickly I almost fall on my ass.

"Fable."

The sound of my name makes me pause, my fingers gripping the edge of the truck door that I was so eager to slam only a second ago. "What?"

"I—I need to process. I need to figure this all out." His eyes implore me to understand. "I need time."

Shaking my head, my chin trembles and I push past it. I refuse to cry in front of him. "How many times do I have to tell you? Don't push me away, Drew."

He inhales deep and looks away from me. That tic is still in his jaw and his expression is so tight, I'm afraid he might shatter. "I don't know how to handle everything with someone else's help. I'm used to coping on my own."

My heart breaks just a little more. I don't know how it's still intact, with everything we've gone through. "Come in with me. I need to check on Owen and then . . . then we can talk. Okay?"

"Owen." His gaze meets mine and he sighs. It's as if he's forgotten everything and I just brought him back to my reality. "Go to your brother. He needs you, too. He's more important right now."

"Drew . . ." Owen is important, he'll always be important, but my worry for Drew matters far, far more. I'm afraid of what he might do if I'm not around.

"Go, Fable. I'll . . . I'll call you."

"No, you won't." Anger fills me and I slam the truck door hard, disappointed at how unsatisfied that still leaves me.

I head toward my apartment building, my shoulders hunched against the light smattering of rain that falls from the dark, angry sky. I hear Drew start up the truck, hear his voice call my name from his open window, but I don't turn around.

I don't answer him.

I do as he says and go to my brother instead.

I stop short when I see my mom sitting on the couch, her eyes bloodshot, her cheeks blotchy. She looks like she's been crying. Owen is standing behind the couch, a helpless expression on his young face, and his eyes fill with relief when he sees me.

"What are you doing here?" I ask her as I shut the door.

She glares at me. "I live here. Where else do you think I'd be?"

Not bothering to say anything, I go to Owen and give him a quick hug. "You all right?"

"Yeah." He slants a nervous glance in Mom's direction. "Now that you're here, do you care if I go over to Wade's for a little bit? I'll be back by dinner, I promise."

"I thought maybe we could go to the movies tonight instead." I so need the distraction. My head is filled with Drew and all the crazy drama that is his life, and I'd prefer to watch a mindless movie for a while and forget.

Though I know that won't really work. How can I ever forget him? Even for a little while.

"I think Mom wants to talk to you." He fidgets. Clearly, he wants to make his escape.

"We'll go to the movies some other time." I ruffle his dark blond hair and he ducks from under my grip, shooting me a winsome smile. "What do you think about having pizza for dinner tonight?"

His face lights up as he heads to the door. "Really? All right!"

I watch Owen leave, turning to Mom when the door shuts behind him. She's watching me warily, her blond hair—so like mine—tumbling over her eyes. Her eyeliner is smudged, her lips pinched. I have a flash in my mind of me looking exactly like this twenty years from now, and the thought alone nearly takes me to my knees.

I refuse to turn into my mother, no matter how similar a path I'm taking to hers.

"Why does he ask you if he can leave and he doesn't ask me?" Mom waves a hand at the closed door. "He acts like you're his mother."

"If you were home more often, then maybe he *would* ask you." I take the duffel bag into my room and dump it onto my unmade bed. I left the place a mess. There are clothes everywhere, I'd left a jumble of cheap jewelry on my old dresser, and the mirror could use a good rubdown with Windex. I use this room to sleep and really for nothing else, since I'm always running around working or doing . . . whatever.

Imagining bringing Drew to my apartment, into my room, I realize he'd probably be disgusted. He's sort of a neat freak, and everyone who lives here is sort of not.

Like I'm ever going to bring him here anyway. There's no way we could work. I need to face facts. He's too damaged, too stubborn to give me a chance.

"I'm home all the time," my mom has the nerve to say when I come back into the living room. She's cracked open a beer and she sips from it, blowing out a harsh breath. "I've had a tough weekend. I don't need you giving me crap to make me feel guilty."

I'd love to hear her definition of a tough weekend. Did they run out of beer or smokes? Maybe her boyfriend flirted with another woman. If anyone has had a tough weekend—hell, a tough fucking week—it's Drew Callahan.

Oh yeah, and me.

"It's only Saturday," I point out. "Don't you have a bar to hang out at or something?"

She snorts. "Since when did you become such a smartass?"

I don't bother answering her. Instead, I head to the tiny kitchen and crack open the fridge, peering inside. It's depressing as hell in there. Leftover Chinese takeout from however long ago and mostly empty bottles of catsup, mustard, mayo, and grape jelly line the door. There's a gallon carton of milk inside, but maybe a sip of it is left and judging by the expiration date printed on there, it's also many days too old.

There are two sodas and a crumpled, half-empty twelve-pack box inside, too. Of course. Heaven forbid Mom goes without her Bud Light.

I vow first thing tomorrow morning, I'll go grocery shopping with the money I made from my girlfriend gig, so we'll have real food in the house. I know Owen's not done growing. He needs to eat and properly, not a bunch of junk shit and fast food. We'll have one last night of cheesy pepperoni pizza, but come tomorrow we're eating right.

"I heard you lost your job," I call to my mother as I grab a soda and crack it open. The cold surge of caffeine and sugar slides easily down my throat and I shut the refrigerator door to find my mom leaning against the kitchen counter, her near-empty beer can hanging from her fingertips.

"Owen told you, huh?" She shakes her head. "It's such bullshit, what they said."

"What did they say?" *Great.* Sounds like it's her fault she lost her job.

"A customer supposedly complained that when I helped him, my breath smelled like beer." She toasts me with her can, then slugs the rest of the beer back. Ironic, much? "I

227

mean, I stayed up late the night before drinking with Larry, so I figure it was a leftover buzz, you know? I wasn't really drunk. I was fine."

I just look at her as I sip from my soda can. My life kinda sucks, my mom is completely irresponsible, but I have nothing on Drew.

Nothing.

"Where's Larry?" When she looks at me, I raise my eyebrows. "Your new boyfriend, right?"

"I don't know." She shrugs. "We got in a huge fight and he dropped me off here not even an hour ago. We were supposed to go out tonight."

God, I really don't want her here. I wish she would go out and leave me alone, leave me with my thoughts. Owen would come back for pizza, but I want to hang out with him. "Maybe you should call Larry and tell him you're sorry."

"Why do you think it's my fault?"

Because it always is? "Maybe you should take the initiative and apologize even if it's not your fault." Now it's my turn to shrug.

Mom taps her lips with her index finger, pulling her cell phone out of her pocket. "Not a bad idea. I'm calling him."

She walks back into her bedroom, her phone to her ear. "Hey, baby. It's me," I hear her say as she slowly closes the door.

I remain where I'm standing long after she's gone. Thinking of Drew. Where is he, what is he doing? Is he okay? I'm sick with worry and I hate feeling this way. I wish he hadn't shut me out. I wish he would let me in.

But wishes are for fools.

Drew

After I drop Fable off at her place, I drive around town for an hour, taking in the familiar, comforting sights. This small town where I've spent the last three years feels far more like home than the place I grew up ever will.

Of course, my hometown is tainted mostly with bad memories, save those few days with Fable.

I drive past the campus, the stadium where I spend the majority of my time, and it's all pretty much abandoned. I drive through downtown, past the shops, the corner cafés and the Starbucks, slowing some as I drive past La Salle's, which looks quiet. Considering it's not even six o'clock, that's no surprise. Plus the students aren't really back in town yet. That'll all happen tomorrow.

The rain still falls steadily and when I realize I've been driving for well over an hour with no destination in mind, I finally end up at my apartment building. It's on the opposite side of town from Fable's; I live in the newer part, the *better* part. Where the neighborhoods are quiet and the yards are perfect. Not like the crowded, older neighbor-hoods that are overrun with young, loud college students since the rents are so cheap. I bet my apartment is twice the size of hers, and I only have one bedroom. Shit, I'm the only one living there, while she has her mom and her brother, all three of them trying their best to keep it to-gether . . .

I hammer my fist against the steering wheel once. Then again, ignoring the pain that radiates across my knuckles, then shoots through my hand. My coach would kill me if he saw me right now, trying to fuck up my throwing hand. Imagining his anger makes me hit the steering wheel yet again, and my fist is throbbing by the third punch.

But the pain feels good. Raw and real, reminding me of who I am, *what* I am. My life looks easy, so damn easy. Everything I've ever wanted has been handed to me on a silver platter. I'm a spoiled-as-hell rich kid who should be living the life. Bragging to my so-called friends, living high in my huge apartment, strutting around campus with a girl under each arm because I'm the one they call the hero, who's saved our football team these last two seasons.

My world . . . is a world of shit. What Adele confessed has left me in fucking shock. I drove pretty much the entire way home without saying a word. Neither did Fable. I feel like shit for acting like that, but what could I do? Make small talk with her, chat about the weather and our favorite music and oh, the fact that my stepmom just told me my sister really wasn't my sister at all, but my *daughter*?

My life is a total soap opera. I don't know how to handle it. I don't know if I believe Adele. She's lied before. She always lies. Maybe she was trying to shock me. Disgust my girlfriend enough to drive her away. My girl is more stubborn than that.

Besides, I know exactly how to drive her away and tune her out. I've become a pro at it these last few days.

That realization fills me with regret.

Unable to stand my out-of-control thoughts any longer, I call Adele while still sitting in my truck in the parking lot, the rain tapping a steady rhythm on the roof.

"Andrew." Adele answers on the second ring, and she sounds surprised to hear from me. She should be.

"Tell me you were lying." The words rush out and I squeeze my eyes closed, waiting—and dreading—her answer.

She's quiet for a moment. I can hear soft music playing in the background, suggesting she's at a restaurant or something. I wonder if she's with my dad. I hope like hell she excused herself so he doesn't hear what she's saying. "I wasn't lying. She belonged to you."

I blow out a harsh breath, my lungs feeling like they're folding in on themselves, they're so tight. "How do you *know*?"

"God, Andrew, it's the same old story, you know? Your father and I . . . we tried for years to have a child, but with no success. The idea came to me one day that you might be the perfect candidate. The next best thing, so to speak, and you were. I planned my visits to you according to my cycle, poked a few holes in the condom, and it was a near-instant success." Her voice is hushed, but she sounds so damn logical about it, I want to scream.

Bile rises in my throat and I swallow it down. I was fucking sixteen years old when I got this bitch pregnant. Only *sixteen*. "So you tricked me. And my father. You've played us both. I hope you're proud of yourself."

"I was never playing either of you—you must believe that. I love your father tremendously. And I . . . I love you, too, Andrew. Can't a woman be in love with two men? There are so many qualities to the both of you that are similar yet different. I wanted you both." Her voice is small. That she even talks about me like she . . . she *wanted* me when I was just a kid makes me sick.

"Well, you had us both. I hope you're satisfied," I snarl into the phone, ready to hang up, but I hear her say my name, her voice downright frantic. I decide to hear her out. I don't know why. "What?"

"You're not . . . you're not going to tell your dad, are you? What I said?"

The knowledge would devastate him. Even if it can't be

confirmed, what with Vanessa gone, I'm not about to blab. Why would I want to hurt him? It would damage our relationship irrevocably and right now, he's the only family I have that counts. This secret, I plan on carrying to the grave. "I won't tell him. Not to save your ass, but to save his."

She exhales loudly, her voice shaky. "Thank you, Andrew."

"Don't bother thanking me. I'm not doing this for you."

"Of course not." She pauses. "What about your— girlfriend? She knows, since I said it in front of her. What if she tells?"

"She won't," I say automatically because I know it's the truth. I trust Fable. She wouldn't dare tell a soul.

"You haven't dated very long. What if you two split up and she becomes vengeful, deciding to ruin both our lives? We might never recover if the truth is revealed." Adele sounds so full of drama, I almost wonder if she gets off on it.

"There's no way in hell Fable will spill this. Stop worrying." And with that, I hang up. I don't want to talk to her anymore. I don't want to talk, period.

Instead, I sit in my truck a little while longer, thinking. The cab gets muggy, the windows steam up from my breathing, and the rain is coming down harder. I don't want to go into my apartment and spend the night there alone. My thoughts are too jumbled, too focused on what Adele said.

I wish she'd never told me the supposed truth about Vanessa. It would've been so much easier to go through life oblivious to that fact.

But she shared in her misery and for that, I'm forever locked to her yet again. Just when I think I'm free of Adele's shackles, she pulls me back in, locks me up.

And tosses away the key.

CHAPTER 16

One week's up, midnight

>*I choose you.*
>—Drew Callahan

Fable

I can't sleep. I'm too restless, too worried, too . . . every-thing. My mom left hours ago after I encouraged her to call her new loser boyfriend to make up with him. He came by within fifteen minutes of her ending the call and they took off to their favorite hangout: a shitty bar the local drunks love.

That I work at a bar doesn't go unnoticed by me. I do realize I'm following in her footsteps no matter how hard I try not to. Makes me wonder if we're predestined to end up like our parents anyway, regardless of whether we fight against it.

Just the thought depresses me, so I file it away.

Owen came home around five, the relief that Mom wasn't there evidenced by his easygoing smile and his teasing—if a little crude—nature. I really need to break him of the bad language habit he's developing at a rapid pace, but who am I to talk? I curse all the fucking time.

We order pizza, and it takes forever because it's the Saturday night after Thanksgiving and no one in town wants to cook. We watch awesome nineties movies on cable—the one luxury I gladly pay for since it makes Owen—okay, fine, and me—happy—and wait for our food, moaning and groaning about how starved we are.

All the while, I think of Drew. His smile, how he touched me, the way he looked at me when he hauled me into his lap that first time. The taste of his lips, the warmth of his breath, the touch of his hands on my bare skin—he haunts me while I tease my brother, as I watch a movie I've seen one hundred times, when I finally shove pizza into my mouth like I haven't eaten for weeks.

I cannot stand the idea of him alone somewhere with his thoughts, his memories, his troubles. I check my phone again and again, hoping for a text, a call, something, but he doesn't contact me. And I won't contact him.

Yet.

Maybe he needs time, I reason with myself later in the

evening as I watch Owen throw some clothes in his back-pack. He's headed back to Wade's to spend the night. His friend called to ask and I spoke with Wade's mom, reas-sured that he really was going over there and not running the streets in the middle of the night. I want to trust my brother, but come on.

He's thirteen.

So I'm left all alone, and I'm used to that. Owen spends the night at his friend's house a lot and my mom prefers staying out until the bars close. I'm always working at night, so no one is usually home around this time anyway.

The rain is still coming down; I can hear it as I lie in my bed in the dark, my eyes wide open as I stare at the ceiling. I can't get Drew out of my mind. I need to know he's okay, that he's safe. Without thought I grab my phone and type in a quick text to him, sending it before I can second-guess myself and delete it.

Slipping out of bed, I go into the living room and curl up on the couch, slinging an old throw blanket over me as I flick on the TV. It's past midnight. Our weeklong fake relationship is officially over.

And as the minutes turn into hours, I realize he's not going to come and rescue me. He kept his word to our agreement.

My position as Drew Callahan's one-week girlfriend is done.

Drew

I passed out cold on top of my bed, still in my jeans and sweatshirt, not bothering to pull the covers over me. I must've slept like that for hours, because I wake up groggy and disoriented, my muscles aching and my mouth dry, my stomach growling since I skipped two freaking meals. I never do that.

Glancing at the alarm clock on my bedside table, I see it's past two in the morning and I sit up, scratch the back of my head, and lean over to flick on the lamp. My cell is sitting on the bedside table, taunting me, and I grab it, push the button to see if anyone called or texted, when I see it. A text from Fable and it says one word.

Marshmallow

Holy shit! She sent it to me hours ago. *Hours.* Feeling like a complete asshole, I practically trip over my feet as I scramble off the bed, shoving my phone in my back pocket and grabbing my keys off the dresser. I should text her back, but that'll take too much time and I'm consumed with the need to see her. I've left her hanging for hours. The thought of disappointing her . . .

I can't stand it.

I leave my apartment and charge out into the still-pouring rain, climb into my truck, and take off. The streets are pretty much empty, I pass only the occasional car, and all I can think about is Fable. Maybe I should've called her. What if she's in real trouble? What if she really needed me and I let her down?

Pulling into her complex's parking lot in record time, I get out of my truck and practically run to her door, remembering the apartment number from picking her up when we left seven days ago.

Damn. I can't believe I've known this girl for only seven days. She's become my everything—and with all my baggage, I've probably become her worst nightmare.

I bound up the concrete stairs to her second-story apartment, the metal railing rattling loudly, and I knock on her door almost frantically, my breath coming in short spurts, the rain dripping down my face.

Long, agonizing minutes go by and I knock again. What if she's not there? Damn it, I definitely should've called first. Pulling out my phone, I'm just about to call when the door cracks open, the safety chain in place.

Relief floods me, making my knees wobble. It's Fable, peering through the narrowly open door, wearing only a thin, oversized T-shirt and nothing else. All I see is long, shapely legs and tousled blond hair.

My body instantly reacts.

"What are you doing here?" Her voice is small. Cold.

"I got your text." I swipe my hand across my face, wiping the raindrops away.

"You're two hours too late." She's about to shut the door but I wedge my foot in, keeping it open. "Go away, Drew."

"Fable, listen to me. I fell asleep. I've been asleep for hours. I woke up not even fifteen minutes ago and the second I saw your message, I hopped in my truck and sped over here." I spread my arms wide. "Look at me. I ran in the fucking rain across my apartment parking lot and yours to get to you."

"So what?" Her flippant tone irritates me. Fable in tough mode is back on full force and I don't like it, though I probably deserve the attitude.

"Come on." I scratch the back of my head. "Just tell me this. Are you all right? Everything okay with your mom and your brother? No crazy emergencies or anything?"

She frowns. "No emergencies. We're fine."

"Good." My heart eases a little and I rub my chest, thankful she's okay. "If you don't want me here, I get it. I just . . . after seeing that text, I had to make sure you were safe."

I ease my foot away so she can close the door and turn, ready to leave, when I hear her speak.

"Drew . . . wait."

Slowly I turn back around to find she's opened the door all the way, allowing me to fully see her. And fuck, she's so beautiful. Her face scrubbed completely of makeup, her expression wary, all that gorgeous hair a wavy mess that tumbles just past her shoulders. The T-shirt only hints at her curves, but I know exactly what she looks like beneath it and my fingers itch to take it off her.

"Yeah?" My voice cracks and I clear my throat. I should stay away from her. Keeping her close brings her into my disastrous world and she has enough problems on her own. She doesn't need mine to royally screw up her life.

"Could you . . . will you come inside and stay with me?"

My heart stills, literally skips a beat, and I take one step forward, ready to leap at this opportunity. Despite the warnings going off in my head, despite knowing I'm not good enough for her, I don't want to turn her away.

I *can't* turn her away. I'm drawn to her. I have to have her. At least one more time before I walk away from her for good. I know it would be in her best interest if I stay out of her life, no matter how selfish I am. But I want to keep her with me.

Forever.

"Where's your mom?" I ask, my voice deceptively casual.

"With her boyfriend."

"And your brother?" I sink my teeth into my lower lip, gnawing at it. I'm this close to doing the right thing and walking away from her.

But I'm also this close to pushing her inside and tearing that shirt right off her tight little body so I can have her naked and beneath me in seconds.

"He's spending the night at his friend's house." She opens the door wider, a clear invitation. "Please, Drew. Come in. You're getting rained on."

She's right. I am. Even with the slight overhang that covers her front door, I'm getting drenched. And it sucks.

"Are you sure you want me?" I ask, my voice low. There's double meaning behind my words. I hope she gets it.

Fable nods slowly, her lips curving into the slightest smile. "I definitely want you."

Without another word, I stride into her apartment, walking right past her. She closes the door and turns the lock as I turn toward her. I slip my arms around her waist and pull her in to me, needing to feel her body as soon as possible.

She surprises me, launching herself at me, her arms going around my neck and her legs curling around my waist. I grab her to keep her in place, my hands gripping her ass. She's wearing flimsy panties, so thin I can feel her warm, pliant flesh, and I groan as she presses her mouth against mine.

We were last together only a few hours ago. Hell, I was inside her body only this morning. But I feel like we've been separated for weeks. Months. Our mouths are ravenous and her hands are buried in my hair, holding me close as I stumble around her living room, finally collapsing on her couch with her still wrapped around me. She's shoving at my sweatshirt, I'm pulling on her T-shirt, and I win the first round, disentangling her from the oversized shirt and whipping it off her body.

She's naked save for the panties, and they don't cover much. My cock is hard as steel as I drink her in greedily, my eyes unable to focus on just one thing. The entire package is gorgeous. Sexy as hell.

And all mine.

Fable scoots closer, lifting her body a little so her breasts are right in my face. She's teasing me, those pretty pale-pink nipples so close to my mouth. I take one in deep, sucking her, swirling my tongue around the hard bit of flesh. She's moaning, grinding her hips against me, her hands clutched tight in my hair, and I slip a hand beneath her panties to stroke her wet flesh.

"Oh God, Drew." She's panting my name, writhing against me while I continue to stroke her. This is nothing like last night, when we took our time and explored each other's bodies.

Right now, I'm frantic, almost out of control with the

need to make her come. She moves her hips against my fingers when I sink them deep, her gaze locking with mine as she parts her lips. A shuddering sigh escapes her and then she's coming, just like that.

Pride suffuses me as I watch her. I'm thinking like an arrogant prick, but damn, that's a turn-on, how easily I just made my girl come.

I carry her into the bedroom, knocking into furniture in the dark, making her giggle as I drop her onto the bed. Her laughter moves through me. She sounds so happy, so carefree, and for a little while, I can pretend I'm the same.

"Take off your clothes," she whispers, her eager voice twisting me up inside, and she's reaching for my jeans, unsnapping and unzipping them quickly. She spreads the parted denim wide and reaches inside, her fingers drifting across the front of my boxer briefs, and I swallow the groan that wants to escape, backing away from her.

She keeps touching me like that and I'll explode.

Shedding my clothes, I grab the single condom that's in the back pocket of my jeans and I slip into the bed with her, gathering her close. She's warm and fragrant and so silky-smooth, I instantly need to be inside her.

"Let me," she whispers, plucking the condom from my fingers and tearing it open. She reaches for me, her slender fingers wrapping around my erection. I roll over on my back and close my eyes, overcome with the sensations her fingers are creating as she slowly strokes me, rolling the condom on so seductively, a shiver steals through my entire body. "I want to be on top," she whispers, and I freeze.

Adele—she almost always wanted to be on top. It didn't bother me to have Fable sitting in my lap when we had sex, but riding me . . . God. I don't know if I can do it.

"Drew." She touches my cheek, startling me, and my eyes meet hers. Even in the darkness, I can see them, shining bright with so much emotion. This girl . . . I still want to claim her as mine, but we said all that stuff last night. Before I knew how much more Adele betrayed me. How much she betrayed our entire family.

I can't subject Fable to this complete mess that's my life. I just . . . *damn*.

I can't.

"I was losing you." She smiles, repeating the very words I said to her last night, and I lean into her palm, turn my face so I can kiss her there. "Let me help you erase the bad memories, Drew. Please?"

"I . . ." Hell, I don't know how to put into words how much this might fuck me up. Not because I'm with her—there's nowhere else I'd rather be, but I'm afraid I might get caught up in the past and do something stupid.

Like push her away. Freak out. Lose my shit completely.

She's already seen you do that and more, yet she's still here. Give her at least this chance.

Reaching for her, I drag her on top of me, her legs straddling my hips. "All right," I whisper, gripping her by her waist, my fingers biting into her skin.

Fable

This quiet moment in my messy bedroom between Drew and me is major. Like, the most important moment between us yet, at least in my eyes.

I'm trying to help him take back his life. Help him forget the past, what Adele—God, I can hardly *think* her name, let alone say it—did to him. I refuse to let the woman have this firm a control over him after all these years. She's not that powerful. I won't let her be.

Keeping my eyes locked with Drew's, I lower myself onto him, a little sigh escaping me as he enters me slowly. Every time our bodies connect, shivers cascade all over my skin and I can't believe it's actually happening. Again. Me. Him.

Together.

His hands are wrapped tight around my waist and I lean forward, brushing my mouth with his. Our eyes are still open as we begin to move and I grip hold of his muscular shoulders, lifting my hips, lowering myself on him and sending him deeper still, until I'm so full of him, I'm overwhelmed completely.

"You feel good," he whispers, rocking into me.

"Keep looking at me." I don't want him to look away. He needs to banish her from his mind completely and focus only on me.

And him. Us. Together.

I've already come once—I was so hot for him, so eager and ready when I realized he actually came to rescue me after all, it didn't take much for his fingers to bring me near-instant pleasure. That orgasm temporarily took the edge off, but I'm foolish to think it would last.

I always want him. Always.

It's always like this between us, too. We come together and we simply . . . combust. So easily. Beautifully. Does he even know how much he affects me? Does he realize how my heart now rests in his hands? I belong to him completely, just as he said last night. None of the bombshells Adele dropped earlier matter. I want to be here for him. Console him, heal him. I want to be his partner in every way.

If he'll let me.

Within moments we're lost so completely in each other. Our skin is damp with sweat as we slide and grind our bodies, swaying in perfect rhythm. The shivery sensations of my second climax already threaten to take me over with his every thrust. I gaze into his eyes, see the desperation, the franticness shading the beautiful blue depths, and I know he's close. So, so close.

"Say my name," I whisper, needing him to know exactly who he's with.

"Fable."

I lift up, pressing my hands against his rock-hard chest, and begin to ride him in earnest. "Say it again," I murmur, closing my eyes for a brief moment, overcome with pleasure.

"*Fable*. God, I'm going to—" He arches into me as he completely loses control and I open my eyes, watch him as he shudders and shakes beneath me. All the while, his eyes are still locked with mine, never breaking the connection, and it's by far the most intimate encounter I've ever experienced with another person.

Collapsing on top of him, I drape my body across his, savoring how our heated skin feels so right pressed together. My head is on his chest, and I can hear his heart beat rapidly against my ear. My eyes close of their own volition when he slides his big hands up and down my back, lulling me, comforting me.

"Thank you," I hear him whisper and I snuggle in close, desperate not to break away from him yet.

"For what?" I need to hear him say it.

"For helping me push her out of my memories." He tugs on my hair and I lift my head, meeting his gaze. "It worked."

I smile lazily, suddenly overcome with exhaustion. "Really?"

"Yeah." He squeezes my butt with his other hand. "I need to get up for a minute. Where's your bathroom?"

I tell him and watch as he climbs off the bed, his naked body so beautiful my chest aches. He goes to the bathroom, disposes of the condom, and is slipping back into my bed within seconds. I pull the covers over us and rest my head on his shoulder, my arm slung across his stomach. "You're staying?"

"Yeah."

He doesn't say anything else and neither do I. I can't. I'm so tired, and it feels so good to fall asleep in Drew's arms. So right. I sleep like the dead, like I did last night when I was also in his arms.

Drew Callahan is as addicting as any sleeping pill.

When I wake up in the morning . . .

He's gone.

CHAPTER 17

A new week, a new life

Fable

Dear Fable,

My worst enemy is behind me because of you.
And there's still a lot left for me to explain.
Right now, all I can think about is you.
So many things in my life confuse me and . . .
Hurt me—except you.
Maybe we can be together again someday.
All I really want is you, but I can't do this now.
Losing you will be the hardest thing I've dealt with
  yet.
Loving you might be a mistake. Drawing you into
  my world will

Only hurt you. And I refuse to do that.
Will you ever forgive me?

I love you.
Drew

My tears fall like raindrops on the letter Drew wrote me, smudging his hastily written words, and I swipe angrily at my cheeks, wiping the tears away. I study the note, trying to make sense of it all. Why would he leave me? Why would he . . .

And then I slowly read the letter again. My heart's racing as I skim the slightly jumbled sentences he wrote just for me, the first letter of each one jumping out at me. I trace every first letter with the tip of my index finger, saying them out loud.

"M-A-R-S-H-M-A-L-L-O-W."

My heart threatens to burst and I clutch the note to my chest. His secret message fills me with so much hope and love, I start to cry all over again. But these tears, they aren't sad. Drew is pushing me away, yet he wants me to rescue him. His letter proves that. But how can I if he won't really let me?

Determination fills me as I carefully fold the piece of paper I found on my bedside table. I open my top dresser drawer, sticking the letter beneath a folded pile of underwear before I slowly hide it away.

Wiping at the corners of my eyes, I stare at my reflection in the mirror. I look different. Older, more mature. Less defiant, less . . . unhappy. Despite the fact that the man I've fallen desperately in love with has left me with a stupid, beautifully heartbreaking note and I've already cried enough tears to fill the kitchen sink, I *am* happy.

Because I know Andrew D. Callahan loves me.

Acknowledgments

To my wondrous critique partner E., who loved the original letter Drew wrote to Fable (and someday, I might just share that sweetly romantic letter) but came up with an even better idea. You save my ass more times than I can count and for that, I will forever be indebted to you. To my husband and kids for putting up with me when I sit at the computer all the livelong day. And to all the readers out there who took a chance on my little story about a damaged boy and a damaged girl: thank you.

Drew and Fable's story isn't over yet!

Read on for a special preview of
Second Chance Boyfriend

Available in trade paperback and eBook
from Bantam Books

CHAPTER 1

Sometimes you have to stand alone, just to make sure
you still can.
—Unknown

Fable

Two months. I haven't seen or heard from him in two freaking months. I mean, who does that to a person? Who spends the most intense week of his life with another human being and shares his most intimate thoughts, his craziest, darkest secrets, has sex with a person—and we're talking amazing, earth-shattering sex—leaves her a note that says I love you, and then bails? I'll tell you who.

Drew *I'm-going-to-kick-him-in-the-balls-next-time-I-see-him* Callahan.

I've moved on. Well, I tell myself that. But time doesn't stop just because my heart does, so I take care of my responsibilities. I've stretched the three thousand dollars I earned for my one week of pretending to be the jerkwad's girlfriend pretty well. I still have some money left in my savings account. I bought my brother, Owen, some cool Christmas gifts. I got my mom something for Christmas, too.

She didn't buy either of us anything. Not one thing. Owen made me a shallow bowl he created in his ceramics class at school. He was so proud to give it to me. A little embarrassed, too, especially when I gushed over it. The kid wrapped it in bright Christmas paper and everything. I was blown away that he took the time to actually create something for me. I keep that bowl on my dresser and leave my earrings in it.

At least someone gives a crap about me, you know?

He didn't give Mom anything. Which—shallow witch that I am—pleased me to no end.

January is supposedly a time of healing. New year, new goals, resolutions, whatever you want to call them, when a person should be hopeful about all that uncharted territory spread out before her. I tried my best to be positive when the new year came, but I cried. That clock struck twelve and I was all by myself, tears running down my face as I watched the ball drop on TV. A pitiful, lonely girl sobbing into her sweatshirt, missing the boy she loves.

Most of the month is gone, and that's fine. But the realization hit me last night. Instead of dreading every single day that comes my way, I need to savor it. I need to figure out what I'm going to do with my life and then actually do it. I'd leave if I could, but I can't ditch Owen. Without me, I have no idea what would happen to him and I can't risk it.

So I stay. I vow to make the best of this life I have. I'm tired of living in misery.

I'm tired of feeling sorry for myself. I'm tired of wanting to shake my mom and make her see that she has children she should give two shits about. Oh, and that she also needs to find a job. Sleeping all day and partying all night with Larry the Loser isn't the way to deal.

And I'm tired of mourning the loss of a beautiful, fucked-up man who haunts my thoughts everywhere I go.

Yeah, I'm most sick of that.

Pushing all mopey thoughts out of my head, I go to the booth where a customer's waiting for me to take his order. He came in a few minutes ago, a blur of a tall man who moved quickly, dressed too nicely for a Thursday mid-afternoon jaunt to La Salle's. The bar is hopping at night, full of college kids drinking themselves into oblivion. But during the day? Mostly bum losers who have nowhere else to go and the occasional person coming in for lunch. The burgers are decent, so they're a draw.

"What can I get you?" I ask once I stop in front of the table, my head bent as I dig out my order pad.

"Your attention, maybe?"

His question—spoken in a velvety deep voice—makes me glance up from my notepad.

Into the bluest eyes I've ever seen. Bluer than Drew's, if that's possible.

"Um, sorry." I offer him a tentative smile. He instantly makes me nervous. He is *waaaay* too good-looking. Like beyond gorgeous, with dark blond hair that falls over his forehead and classic bone structure. Strong jaw, sharp cheekbones, straight nose—he could've walked right off a billboard. "Are you ready to order?"

He smiles, revealing even white teeth, and I clamp my lips shut to prevent them from falling open. I didn't know men could be this attractive. I mean, Drew is gorgeous—I can admit that even though I'm furious at him. But this guy . . . he puts all other men to shame. His face is too damn perfect.

"I'll take a Pale Ale." He flicks his chin at the tattered menu lying on the table in front of him. "Anything from the appetizer menu you can recommend?"

He must be joking. Beyond the burgers, I wouldn't recommend any food La Salle's serves to this ideal male specimen. Heaven forbid it might taint him. "What are you in the mood for?" I ask, my voice weak.

Lifting a brow, he picks up the menu and glances it over, his gaze meeting mine. "Nachos?"

I shake my head. "The beef is rarely cooked all the way." More like it comes out with a pink tinge. So gross.

"Potato skins?" He winces.

I wince back. "So nineties, don't you think?"

"How about the buffalo wings?"

"If you want to set your mouth on permanent fire. Listen." I glance around, making sure no one—as in my boss—is nearby. "If you want something to eat, I suggest the café down the street. They have great sandwiches."

He laughs and shakes his head. The rich, vibrant sound washes over me, warming my skin, followed quickly by a huge dose of wariness. I don't react like this to guys. The only other one who could earn this sort of reaction from me is Drew. And he's not around . . . so why am I still so hung up on him?

Maybe because you're still in love with him, like some sort of idiot?

I shove the nagging little voice that pops up at the most inopportune times into the back of my brain.

"I like your honesty," the man says, his cool blue gaze raking over me. "I'll just take the beer, then."

"Smart decision." I nod. "I'll be right back."

I head toward the back and slip behind the bar, grab-bing a bottle of Pale Ale, glancing up to catch the guy staring at me. And he doesn't look away, either, which makes me feel uncomfortable. He's not watching me like a pervert, he's just very . . . observant.

It's unnerving.

A trickle of anger flickers through me. Do I wear an invisible sign around my neck? One that says *Hey, I'm Easy*? Because I'm not. Yeah, I made a few mistakes, looking for attention in the wrong places, but it's not like I dress with my tits or ass hanging out. I don't put any sort of purposeful swing to my hips, nor do I thrust my chest out the way I see plenty of girls do.

So why does every guy I encounter seem to blatantly check me out like I'm a piece of meat?

Deciding I've had enough of his crap, I stride toward his table and set the beer in front of him with a loud clunk. I'm about to walk away without saying a word—screw the tip—when he asks, "So what's your name?"

I glance over my shoulder. "What's it matter to you?" Oh, I'm such a bitch! I could really piss this guy off and get myself fired. I don't know what's wrong with me.

I'm almost as bad as my mom. She sabotaged her job with her drinking and her awful attitude. At least I only have the bad attitude.

If I could kick my own ass, I would be doing so right now.

He smiles and shrugs, as if my smart-ass remark doesn't faze him. "I'm curious."

Turning fully, I face him, studying him as intently as he studies me. The long fingers of his right hand are wrapped around the neck of the beer bottle, his other arm resting on the scarred and scratched table. His entire manner is relaxed, easy, and my defenses slowly lower.

"It's Fable," I admit, bracing for the reaction. I've heard endless jokes and rude remarks about my name since I can remember.

But he doesn't give me a hard time. His expression remains neutral. "Nice to meet you, Fable. I'm Colin."

I nod, not knowing what else to say. He both puts me at ease and shakes me up, which leaves me confused. And he definitely doesn't fit in at this bar. He's dressed too nice and has an air of authority about him that borders on entitlement, as if he's above it all—and he probably is. He reeks of class and money.

But he's not acting like an ass and he should, I've been so rude to him. He brings the beer bottle to his lips, taking a drink, and I watch unabashedly. He's handsome. He's arrogant. And he's trouble.

I don't want anything to do with him.

"So, Fable," he says once he's downed half his beer. "Can I ask you a question?"

Shuffling my feet, I glance around the bar. No one's paying us any attention. I could probably stand here and talk to Colin the mysterious customer for fifteen minutes and no one would protest. "Sure."

"Why is a woman like you working in a shit bar like this?"

"Why is a guy like you ordering a beer in a shit bar like this?" I retort, momentarily insulted. But then I realize . . . he's complimenting me. And he referred to me as a woman. No one ever does that. *I* don't do that.

He tips his beer at me, as if offering a toast. "Touché. Would you be surprised if I said I came in here looking for you?"

Surprised? More like creeped out. "I don't even know you. How could you be looking for me?"

"I should rephrase that. I came here hoping I would find someone I could steal away." At my raised eyebrows, he laughs. "I own a new restaurant in town. The District. Have you heard of it?"

I had. Some fancy new place that caters to the rich college kids, the ones with an endless supply of money they can use to eat, drink, and party. So not my scene. "Yeah."

"Have you been there?"

I slowly shake my head. "No."

Leaning back against the seat, he studies me, his lids heavy as he does a slow perusal of . . . me. Now he's totally checking me out and I can feel my cheeks burn with embarrassment. The guy is sort of a jackass.

I've always had a slight thing for jackasses.

"Come with me to the restaurant tonight. I'll show you around." His mouth curves into not quite a smile and I'm tempted.

But I've also sworn off men, so I know this is a bad idea. "Thanks, but I'm not interested."

"I'm not trying to ask you out on a date, Fable," he says, his voice low, his eyes glowing. I take a step back, glancing around. I need to get away from this guy. Fast. But then his words stop me in my tracks. "I'm trying to offer you a job."

Drew

"Let's talk about Fable."

I tense up but nod. I try my best to appear neutral, like our new topic of discussion doesn't bother me. "What do you want to know?"

My shrink watches me, her careful gaze steady. "It still bothers you to hear her name."

"It doesn't," I lie. I try my best to appear nonchalant, but my insides are churning. I both dread and savor hearing Fable's name. I want to see her. I *need* to see her.

Yet I can't make myself go to her. And she's clearly given

up on me. I deserve her giving up. I gave up on her first, didn't I?

More like you gave up on yourself.

"You don't have to lie to me, Drew. It's okay if it's still difficult." Dr. Sheila Harris pauses, tapping her index finger against her chin. "Have you considered trying to see her?"

I shake my head. I consider it every day, every minute of my life, but my considerations are useless. "She hates me."

"You don't know that."

"I know *I'd* hate me for what I did if I were her. I shut down and shut her out, like I always do. She begged me again and again not to do it. Promised that she'd be there for me no matter what." Yet I left her. With only a stupid note that took me way too long to write, filled with a secret message that my smart, beautiful girl figured out right away.

But she's not my girl. I can't lay claim to her. I ignored her. And now . . .

I've lost her.

"So why did you shut her out? You've never told me, you know."

My psychologist loves to ask the tough questions; but that's her job. I still hate answering them. "It's the only way I know how to cope," I admit. The truth slaps me in the face on a daily basis. I always run.

It's so much easier.

I sought Dr. Harris out myself. No one else pushed me to do it. After we came back from Carmel, after I ditched Fable and left her that bullshit note, I withdrew into myself worse than ever. I fucked up my game play. I fucked up my grades. Winter break came and I ran away. I literally ran away to some crazy cabin in the middle of the woods I rented from some nice old couple in Lake Tahoe.

My plan? Hibernate like a bear. Turn off my phone, hole up by myself, and figure my shit out. I didn't anticipate how hard it would be, though, being alone with my thoughts. My memories, both the good and the bad, haunted me. I thought of the bombshell my stepmom, Adele, dropped on me. I thought about my dad and how much the truth—if it really is the truth—would affect him. I thought about my little sister, Vanessa, and how she died. How she might not be my little sister after all . . .

More than anything, I thought of Fable. How mad she'd been when I showed up on her doorstep, yet she let me in anyway. The way I touched her, how she touched me, the way she always seemed to break down my barriers and see the real me. I let her in. I *wanted* to let her in.

And then I left her. With a note that was rendered pointless because she tried her damnedest to rescue me and I wouldn't let her. She sent me exactly two texts. The second one surprised me, because I figured she was stubborn and I thought she'd give up after I didn't answer the first one.

How could I answer it, though? She said all the right things. And I would've said all the wrong things. So it's better to say nothing at all.

She also left me one voice mail. I still have it. Sometimes, when I'm feeling really fucked-up, I play it. Listen to her soft, tearful voice, those unbelievable words she says to me. By the time the message is finished, my heart literally hurts.

It's torture listening to it, yet I can't make myself delete that message, either. Just knowing it's there, that for one last minute she actually cared, is better than deleting those words and her voice and pretending she doesn't exist.

"I'm hoping to help you with that. Your coping mechanisms," Dr. Harris says, drawing me out of my thoughts. "I know how much she means to you. Fable. And I'm hoping that eventually, you'll go to her and tell her you're sorry."

"What if I'm not sorry?" I toss the words out, but they're meaningless. I'm so sorry I can't begin to explain how much of a screw-up I am.

"Then that's another issue we'll have to deal with," she says gently.

It goes on like this for another fifteen minutes and then I finally make my escape, walking out into the cold, clear winter afternoon. The sun is warm on my skin despite the temperature and I start down the sidewalk, heading for where I parked my truck. Harris's office is downtown, in a nondescript building, and I hope like hell I don't see anyone I know. The college campus is only a few blocks away and students hang out at the little stores, cafés, and coffee shops that line the street.

It's not like I have many friends, but hell. Everyone likes to think they know me. No one really does. With the exception of one person.

"Hey, Callahan, wait up!"

Pausing, I glance over my shoulder to see one of my teammates running toward me, a big grin on his goofy face. Jace Hendrix is a pain in the ass but generally a good guy. He's never done me wrong, not that any of them ever really have. "Hey." I offer him a wave and shove my hands into my jacket pockets, waiting until he stops just in front of me.

"Long time, no see," Jace says. "You sort of disappeared after that last failure of a game."

I wince. That last failure of a game had been all my fault. "I was feeling sort of fucked-up over that," I confess.

Hell, I can't believe I just admitted to my failures, but Jace doesn't seem bothered. "Yeah, you and everyone else, man. Listen, what are you doing this weekend?"

The way Jace brushes off my statement—hell, the way he agrees with it—blows me away. "What's going on?"

"It's Logan's birthday. We're doing it up right at the

new restaurant that just opened a few blocks over. Have you heard of it?" Jace looks excited, he's literally bouncing on his feet, and I wonder what the hell is up.

"Vaguely." I shrug. Like I care. The last thing I want is to be social.

But then Dr. Harris's words ring through my head. How she wants me to reach out. And act like a real person.

"Party's going to be there. I haven't been there yet, but I hear all the waitresses are gorgeous, the drinks are delicious and loaded with alcohol, and Logan's parents arranged for a private room. Rumor has it strippers might've been hired out for this momentous event. Logan's turning twenty-one, so we want to get him all sorts of fucked-up." Jace waggles his eyebrows.

"Sounds great," I lie. It sounds like torture. But I need to go. At the very least, make a quick appearance and then scram. I can report back to my shrink what I did. She can give me a gold star for making an effort.

"You'll go?" Jace looks shocked, and I know why. I rarely do anything with the guys, especially in the last few months, when I've been like a ghost.

"I'll be there." I nod, unsure how I'm going to work up the energy to make an appearance, but I've got to do this.

"Yeah? Awesome! I can't wait to tell the guys. We've missed you. Haven't seen you for a while, and we all know those last few games were tough on you. They were tough on all of us." Jace's expression is solemn, and for a minute I wonder if he's playing my ass.

But then I realize he's sincere. Funny how I took full responsibility for those losses when I bet every single one of these guys on my team probably did the same thing.

"Tell the guys I can't wait to see them." The words fall easily from my lips because they're the truth. I need to stop wallowing in my own misery. I need to stop worrying about my past, worrying about my dad and my bitch of a stepmom and the little girl who died because I was too busy fighting with her mom and telling her to keep her goddamn hands to herself.

That's the one regret I have, that I never fully explained to Fable what happened that day. I know she assumes I was off screwing around with Adele. I would think the same. But that was the day I told her never again. Whatever she was going to try, I wasn't interested. It was over. That was the day I became liberated.

And also the day I became a prisoner of my own guilt.

Forever.

"See ya around, Drew." Jace waves and turns, whistling as he walks away from me. I remain rooted to the spot, watching him leave until he's a speck of nothing in the distance, wishing like crazy I could be that carefree.

That my biggest concerns were my grades, what girl I could get my hands on next, and how excited I was for the big party coming up in a few days.

Maybe, just maybe, I could lose myself in the mundane for a bit. Pretend that nothing else matters but friends and school and parties. Doc says I can't move forward until I face the past.

But what the fuck does she know?

PHOTO: COLBY RAIMER

New York Times and *USA Today* bestselling author MONICA MURPHY is a native Californian who lives in the foothills below Yosemite. A wife and mother of three, she writes new adult contemporary romance and is the author of *One Week Girlfriend* and *Second Chance Boyfriend*.

www.monicamurphyauthor.com
missmonicamurphy@gmail.com
www.facebook.com/MonicaMurphyauthor
www.facebook.com/DrewAndFableOfficial
www.twitter.com/MsMonicaMurphy